A TASTE OF ASHES

A TASTE OF ASHES

Tony Black

BLACK & WHITE PUBLISHING

First published 2015
by Black & White Publishing Ltd
29 Ocean Drive, Edinburgh EH6 6JL

1 3 5 7 9 10 8 6 4 2   15 16 17 18

ISBN   978 1 84502 964 7

A CIP catalogue record for this book is available from the British Library.

ALBA | CHRUTHACHAIL

Typeset by RefineCatch Ltd, Bungay, Suffolk
Printed and bound by Nørhaven, Denmark

For Cheryl and Conner

ACKNOWLEDGEMENTS

I'd like to thank Dr Robert Ghent for his assistance, once again, in helping with the medical research. And to all at Black & White Publishing for making the process run so smoothly.

1

Agnes Gilchrist hid behind the open curtain in her front room. She'd seen some of her neighbours rushing by, grimacing, sneering at the window as they passed. When the new bus stop went in and the unruly wee brats from both ends of the street started to treat it like a gang hut, stones were thrown at her window. She called the police then, they knew her name now.

Frank was more cautious, worried about people's opinions. He complained if she spent her time at the window, watching what went on in the street. But now he wasn't there to complain, to tell her to get out in the world, get on with her life and leave others to theirs.

Agnes moved away from the curtain, she folded up Frank's good suit, the brown tweed one, and put it in the carrier bag for the charity shop collection. Someone would get a wear out of it. She peered at the window once more, it was starting up again.

'What a racket,' she said.

Number 23 were a rowdy lot, even for this end of Whitletts. She couldn't decide whether it had been worse with the police cars round every night of the week, before that boy joined the army. It might have been, but then was there a time when it had been truly quiet?

'What in the name of God?'

Shouts and screams. Another disturbance. Even the mobile butcher didn't park there now – he said it affected trade because no one wanted to queue up where a full-scale row was likely to break out at any minute. 'You don't want to see the chip pan coming through the window when you're only out for a pound of mince!' was his comment last week.

'Animals.' That's what Frank called them. Things were better in his day, though. The Millars at 23 had got worse lately.

'It'll be herself rowing with the fancy man.'

Agnes reached for the telephone, pulled the chord to her, and when the receiver was within reach she placed her bony hand on it.

Shouting again. Screaming. The woman sounded hysterical now.

Agnes's heart fluttered as she tightened her grip on the telephone. She lifted the receiver, made sure the line was working, and then lowered it again.

Everything went silent now. This was an unusual turn. Normally the rows went on for hours until there was some final act like a door slamming or a police car pulling up.

'Oh, here we go.'

The door opened and a figure, pressed against the wall, eased silently into the night. Agnes squinted to see what was going on but there wasn't enough light. The street lamps, smashed and never replaced, were no help in identifying the figure. She followed its stealthy trail into the

2

shadows at the end of the road then returned her gaze to the house.

A woman, illuminated by the light from the hallway behind her, was sobbing on the front step. She was shaking; even at this distance that was visible. It was Sandra Millar, her face clearing into view every time she threw back her head.

'He'll have left her, that'll be it.'

Agnes checked herself for sympathy – once she would have reached out, went over and offered to put the kettle on – but times had changed. These days you were more likely to be roared at, told not to interfere, and pointed back to your own door.

But Sandra Millar was truly in distress. The wailing and sobbing growing louder than it ever had before. Was she injured, in pain? The stories you heard these days, the things people did to each other. The old woman's instincts begged her to get help.

'Hello, police.' She told the girl on the emergency line what she had just seen.

The operator recorded the details, was a kind enough sort. 'There'll be a patrol car around soon, just sit tight now.'

'But what about herself? She's in an awful state.'

'I'd recommend you sit tight, just stay where you are until the police arrive.'

'Right, OK.'

'Would you like me to stay on the line with you?'

'No, it's all right.' Her curiosity lingered.

'Are you sure? Maybe just till the police get there.'

3

'No, it's fine. I'll be fine.'

Agnes returned the telephone to its resting place and drew back the curtain once more, but as she saw Sandra holding her head in her hands she was compelled to go to her. She headed for the door and down the front steps, as she approached number 23 she heard low wails like a wounded animal. Agnes's fluttering heart quickened, started to pound.

'Hello, is everything all right?'

There was no answer. The sobbing stopped instantly. As the woman saw her neighbour's approach, her mouth widened and her white face tightened in pain. She tried to scream, but the sound was trapped in her. She jolted upright and dashed into the house, heading for the kitchen. The door battered the wall, swung wildly, then she appeared again and bolted for the garden. She ran for the road and didn't look back once.

Agnes's breathing halted, she was cold. A chill breeze blew but that wasn't the reason her temperature dropped. Beyond the doorway she peered into the fully-lit hallway and gathered her cardigan tight to her shoulders. The place was silent, appeared to be empty. She saw the wall-mounts with their smashed glass lying on the floor, and a smeared line, long and dark, running down the white wall towards the kitchen. She followed the smear-line like a pointer all the way to the next open door, to the sight of the kitchen table where he sat with a large wound above his shoulder blades and blood pooling on the well-worn linoleum beneath.

It took the old woman's eyes a few moments to decipher

4

the image in front of her and then the shock sent a shiver through her tensed body. Her knees loosened quickly as she fell into the open door, making a light thud as her delicate frame collapsed on the hard floor.

2

As Detective Inspector Bob Valentine left the station the red wash of sky was sinking into a jagged grey horizon. The King Street flats blocked most of the scene and allowed only a dim hum from the swelling traffic beyond. In the early evening, Ayr's atmosphere pulsed with rushing commuters fleeing cramped offices. Previously sluggish limbs bursting with new energy. It was a time of day that never ceased to fascinate the detective, a strange place between the working world and the coming darkness that gave cover to a more sinister night.

Night crimes were always different from the affairs of daylight hours. If it sounded superstitious, supernatural even, then Valentine accepted it without a shrug. By this stage he knew the facts and they couldn't be ignored, it would be a fool who tried. DI Bob Valentine knew he was no fool, at least when it came down to the job. In what remained of his life outside the force, he conceded, the opposite was likely to be true.

The silver Vectra was filthy, muddy arches and a roof covered in thick, mucky dust. The detective ran his finger along the dull wing and frowned. 'Could write my name in that.'

He'd told DS McAlister to take the car for a wash and

wax earlier but obviously he hadn't barked loud enough for the importance of the request to register. 'Bloody hell, Ally,' he shook his head. 'Tonight of all nights.'

Valentine opened the back door of the car and flung his briefcase in the footwell. As he removed his jacket a bead of sweat prickled on his brow, he dabbed at it with the back of his hand, settled behind the wheel and started the engine. The police radio was on, fizzed a little, then spluttered a message for uniform.

'Getting reports of a disturbance on Arthur Street at the Meat Hangers nightclub, anyone available to attend?'

The detective leaned over and turned off the radio. The call was only a short diversion away, but it might as well have been a hundred miles.

'No chance.' He gripped the wheel.

It was a mild night, a slight breeze but nothing serious. One of those evenings where he was glad to be on the west coast; at the tail end of spring the west's worst offence was mugginess blurring the views across the Firth of Clyde to the Isle of Arran. In the summer he'd heard you could grow tomatoes outside because of the warm winds of the Gulf Stream, though he had never tried. The idea of himself as a gardener was enough to make him laugh; days of domesticity, of normalcy, were not for him. He checked his wristwatch – at least he was on time – he might not arrive in a gleaming car but he'd arrive nonetheless. It would be a small victory to weigh against the deepening shame he had come to feel for his position as a family man who spent so little time at home.

Valentine drove to the edge of Barns Street and parked

the car. The crimson sky was retreating behind a widening grey smear now, but it didn't seem to bother the runners and dog walkers descending on the Low Green. In a few months the grass would be dotted with day-trippers clutching disposable barbecue sets and – the scourge of uniform – teenagers with two-litre bottles of cider. The detective drew a deep breath; his own daughter was just about old enough to be one of them. The thought that Chloe was of an age to experiment with drink, and more besides, made his insides tense.

The Vectra's side-lights blinked as Valentine locked up and headed for the Gaiety Theatre. He checked his watch again, he was still on time, the idea that he wouldn't be – after Chloe's months of pestering – was unthinkable. Clare had already warned him about missing their daughter's stage debut and Valentine regarded his daughter as too precious to disappoint. He made for the theatre, brushing the shoulders of his jacket with his fingertips as he went. Something like pride – he remembered it now – was sneaking back into his consciousness.

In the foyer, Valentine collected his ticket and made for the stairs. The atmosphere unnerved the detective, he wasn't used to mahogany panelling – even the slightly worn variety of the Gaiety's – it was an industrial shade of grey that covered the walls of King Street station. Perhaps more concerning than the setting, however, was that he would have to spend the next hour and a half with his phone switched off; he could never fully outrun the job.

Clare spotted him first, leaning out from her seat in the middle of the row and beckoning him to her.

'Hello,' he muttered under heavy breath.

As Valentine entered the narrow seating channel he was forced to dislodge some sneering early birds.

Clare stepped in front of him when he drew near. 'You're here. I had wondered.'

'I said I was coming.'

'Yes, but you say lots of things, Bob.'

His father rose beside her, coughing loudly as if to distract Clare. She turned. 'I know, I know – we're here to enjoy ourselves.'

'Hello, Dad.' He watched the old man sway a little, stooped where he stood. 'Sit down, I'm here now.'

His father had scraped back his thinning hair and wore a dark suit, the same one he wore to Bob's mother's funeral. 'You scrub up not too bad, Dad.'

'It's not every night your own take to the stage.'

Clare brightened beside him; Valentine took a moment to share in their pride. 'Where's Fiona?'

'Buying sweets, there's a queue.'

There was an awkward silence when the three stared ahead at the empty stage, and then the old man spoke. 'I think I'll go and find some mints myself, they used to have a wee girl that sold peanuts and cigarettes but I suppose they've long done away with her.'

'She'll be pensioned off now, Dad.'

'Cheeky bugger, it wasn't that long ago.' He paused as he stood. 'Actually maybe it was, can I get you pair anything?'

They shook their heads and watched until he was out of sight. As the old man left them, Clare jerked herself to face Valentine. 'I swear, if you do anything to ruin tonight for

9

our daughter your murder squad won't have to look far for their next victim.'

'Harsh, Clare.' He returned her gaze. 'I'm here aren't I? Like I said I would be.'

'I hope that phone's off.'

The standard response sat on his lips – a desire to defend himself – but it wasn't the place. 'It's switched off, yes.' Valentine treated his wife to a wide smile. He turned away, started to remove his jacket and use it to fashion a buffer between himself and any more strife.

'You look nice, dear.'

Clare peered over her nose. 'Yes, it's a new dress if that's what you're getting at!'

'No, I never said a thing.' He took in the dress. 'It's very nice though, you suit it.'

She crossed her legs, there was a sharp edge to her voice. 'And the shoes are new too, before you ask.'

'I wasn't about to.' Clare's unease was down to the fact that there were too many previous occasions he hadn't been there for his daughters. He couldn't blame her for the reaction, it was justified. Clare was the homebuilder, his contributions were minimal.

The chatter in the auditorium started to subside, a new hush spreading. As Valentine peered along the row his father and daughter appeared clutching bags of sweets, their hands were full.

'Fiona, you'll make yourself sick if you eat that lot,' said Clare.

'She's fine, it's a one-off.' Valentine reached over to help his daughter into her seat. 'Hello, love.'

Clare whispered as he stretched passed her, 'Good cop, bad cop is it?'

He let the comment go, turned back to face the stage. 'Must be starting.'

'It's a bit early.' Clare checked her watch, curtains seemed to be moving on the stage. 'Hang on, what's this?'

Valentine followed the line of his wife's fingernail as she pointed to the side of the stage. A broad man in a white shirt and black tie was peering from the edge of the curtain, he was theatre staff, but the man with him wasn't.

'Oh, Christ.'

'What?' Clare turned towards her husband. 'What is it?'

As the detective stared out he recognised the figure beside the theatre usher, there was no mistaking the gangly frame beneath the well-worn wax jacket.

'It's Ally.'

Clare's face drooped. 'Who?' She jerked her gaze back towards the stage. The usher was pointing to their row now, the man in the wax jacket easing himself down the stage and jogging towards the middle aisle.

'Tell me this isn't happening,' said Clare.

Valentine searched for a response but found none. He turned towards his wife and garbled, 'Something's up. I don't know what. Look, I'm sorry.'

Ally appeared out of breath before them. He nodded first to Clare, then to Valentine. 'Hello, boss, we've got a live one, I'm afraid.'

'A live what, Ally?'

The DS leaned over, lowered his voice. 'Erm, maybe what I should have said was we've got a dead one.'

3

As Valentine rose from his chair, retrieved his coat, Clare sat with her arms folded tight across her chest. If there was a glimmer of sympathy lurking in her for the fact that he was going to miss their daughter's big night, Valentine couldn't find it. He'd angered her by doing the one thing he promised that he wouldn't do – put the job first, again.

The detective stood for a moment, fastening his coat, and trying to locate a crack in the stonewall Clare had built around herself, but it was useless. Her anger was one thing, merely the outward projection of her inner hurt, it was the upset he'd caused that dug at his conscience and made him want to plead forgiveness.

'Look, Clare . . .'

She cut in. 'Leave it.'

'I'm sorry, I have to . . .'

'Just go, will you.'

Valentine looked at DS McAlister – who had the good grace to avert his gaze and remove himself from the scene – he stood biting the inside of his cheek and tapping his foot. He was attracting the attention of the theatre goers, who were turning and staring, whispering to each other in wonder at the strange break in proceedings.

'Right, I'll call, Clare.' She didn't move. As he left Valentine caught a glimpse from his father that indicated he might try and talk to his wife; it wasn't an optimistic look.

Valentine followed the DS to the car park, there were too many people milling about inside the theatre for him to ask why he was being dragged away from his family. As the cooler air outside worked on his temperament the detective breathed deeply and tried to compose himself – it would have been too easy to get mad with Ally, too familiar a routine as well; whether it was age or experience keeping him composed, however, he didn't know.

'OK, son, tell me what's what. Not the nightclub on Arthur Street is it? I heard it on the radio on the way in.'

Ally kept walking towards his car. As he pointed the keys the sidelights flashed. 'No, that's a hold-up, would you believe? DI Eddy Harris is all over it.'

'Flash Harris, that fits . . . It was a jeweller's last week, Ayr's turning into bloody Dodge City. OK, so what have we got, then?'

'Hard to say what the situation is at present, boss. All we know is it's a bloke who's taken a blade in the back and his claret's all over the kitchen floor. We taking my car, yeah?'

Ally's casual tone was customary among the squad but didn't fool Valentine. He knew if they had a murder on their patch then every one of his team would be focused – it didn't stop him teasing the DS. 'You make it sound like one for that *Kitchen Nightmares* show.'

Ally allowed himself a grin, by the time they got inside

13

the car he had upgraded to a laugh. 'Those celebrity chefs are a joke, think they'd try on that hard-man patter in real life? Wouldn't be five minutes before some psycho was tenderising the Botox out their face.' The car's engine spluttered, the wheels turned on the tarmac.

Valentine spoke: 'Am I going to have to batter the details of this case out of you, Ally?' They were at the bus garage, turning onto the Sandgate. 'Where are we going for a start, son?'

'Whitletts, boss.'

The DI nodded. 'It just doesn't get any better does it?'

'No, sir. It's the junkies isn't it? I heard some statistic the other day that nearly forty per cent of the houses up there have a drug dependent.'

'Is this a drugs killing, or are you just trying to make me think you actually read the background reports that cross your desk?'

'I don't know much more than I've told you.' The King Street station came into view, lights glowing inside creating the appearance of industry. 'Looks busy, boss. Think we'll be burning the midnight oil tonight?'

Having to pull a late shift at the station on the night his eldest daughter had made her stage debut, as the rest of the family were celebrating, crushed Valentine. The feeling passed quickly, though, as his sense of duty was renewed by the situation. There had been a murder in his hometown, and that was something he could never ignore. Whatever was stacking up at home, none of it compared to the need for justice. That would never change because it was the other side of his devotion to his family:

14

if anything happened to them, he would expect no less than the kind of retribution only someone like him could deliver.

'Ally, when's the most important part of an investigation?'

The DS glanced in Valentine's direction. 'Have I said something wrong?'

'The first twenty-four hours, son. Forty-eight hours at a push. After that we're onto extrapolating the known facts and, not a favourite of mine, guesswork.'

'I think I see what you're getting at.'

'You do? Good.' Valentine pointed to a gap in the road where a row of police cars had parked up, he had the car door open before the vehicle stopped. As the brakes halted the wheels, he pushed himself from the car and motioned with a curled index finger for DS McAlister to follow promptly. On the pavement he was met by a crowd of noisy residents. The noisiest – a woman in sweatpants and a housecoat who was shadowed by two hyperactive youngsters – fronted up to him, blocking the path. 'You going to tell us what's going on?'

Valentine sidestepped the woman without an answer and one of the children, a young boy in football colours, started up the path after him. 'Get those children inside, please. This is a police investigation.'

As Valentine halted his stride, turned, DS McAlister directed the woman back towards the crowd on the side of the road. She wrested her arm from his grip. 'Get your mitts off me, it's a free country, you pig.'

'It won't be free for you if I arrest you,' McAlister snapped back.

'Arrest me for what?' Her mouth drooped open, a gap-toothed glower that said she might just be stupid enough to test the officer.

'How about disrupting a police investigation?' His tone was flat, fully controlled. 'Or maybe I'll just do you for civil disobedience. Now get indoors, all of you.'

Valentine provided backup. 'I'll have officers round to speak to you all as soon as possible. But in the meantime please go home and let us get on with our work. There's nothing to be gained from hanging about on the street, and it's cold! Come on, take the kiddies indoors.'

The woman sunk back from the officers, pushed open the gate at the end of her garden. The crowd started to disperse. DS McAlister approached Valentine as he lengthened his stride towards the property. 'That was a close one,' he said.

'They're just scared. They know something's happened, and on their own doorstep, I wouldn't want that any more than them.'

'Aren't you worried about contamination of the crime scene? About kids running all over the evidence.'

The DI fought back an urge to ridicule McAlister for swatting him with the textbook. 'Ally, you have to treat people like people. That's your first and foremost. But it's a fair point, why don't you get uniform to put up a cordon?'

'I'll do that and if anyone crosses it, I'll make sure they're thrown in the divvy van, in full view of their pals.'

Valentine stamped towards the murder scene. 'And when you're done building community relations, come and join the rest of the squad in there,' he pointed to the front door of the house, 'slight matter of a murder investigation to get under way.'

4

The path to the house was clogged with bodies, the SOCOs in their restrictive white suits being the most obvious. The officers in uniform were almost as prevalent but the others in plain clothes were only identifiable as part of the squad by their industry. As Valentine got closer he noticed that an assortment of little yellow A-boards littered the path. They sat next to the familiar shapes made by blood droplets falling on concrete. It fell flat and round, splayed and squashed, it lay as innocuous as red paint but he knew it was not. The blood pools delineated a shambling route that led to the gate and then seemed to have been lost on the black tarmac of the pavement and road.

The detective halted to take in the sweep of the street. Beyond the place he had ran into the welcoming party of neighbours there was a grassy patch, its edges eroded into a muddy thoroughfare, and further on a disconsolate copse of trees. Beyond that was the main road, the town of Ayr, and from there more possibilities than he could count. He turned back, looked the other way up the street: there was a badly scarred bus shelter, the unbreakable Perspex windows melted into holes by determined vandals. The sight held his interest for a second before he returned to the grassy patch: four houses, terraced, between the murder scene and the short cut to the town centre. If he'd been a murderer himself, he would have gone that way. Of course, if he'd been planning it properly, there would have been a car – at that hour of the evening the sound of a car's engine was not unfamiliar – but this was Whitletts. This was an area where murder wasn't planned, not in that way; in places like this, murder festered over years and months and then appeared, fully blown, like it was pre-ordained to happen. The consequences were an afterthought at best. They were at worst – and most likely on this occasion – something to run away from as quickly as possible.

DS Sylvia McCormack emerged from the garden where she had been directing officers in a search, as she approached the detective she waved with a pair of rubber gloves. 'Hello, sir, sorry to drag you away, hope it wasn't anything special.'

Valentine didn't want to be reminded of just how special his plans had been this evening but let it pass. 'What's the SP, Sylvia?'

'Well, we have a white male, late-forties-to-fifties, with a deep wound at the base of the neck. Dead, of course.'

'He'd bloody want to be for all this fuss.' The DI walked towards the front door. On the step he paused to point out some medical paraphernalia, needles and phials. 'Did the paramedics get to him before he carked?'

'Eh, no, that was for . . .' she removed a spiral-bound notebook from her coat pocket, read from the page, 'Agnes Gilchrist, a neighbour.'

'Stumbled on the scene, so we have a witness?'

DS McCormack turned another page in her notebook, she was looking for the answer but it wasn't there. 'She was unconscious on arrival, sir.'

'*On our arrival*, Sylvia. But not *her* arrival. I'm assuming somebody called emergency for us to be here in the first place, was it her?'

McCormack lowered her gaze, retrieved a pencil and started to write on the notebook. 'I'll get that checked out, right away.'

Valentine let a moment's silence sit between them. 'Thanks, Sylvia, it might turn out to be important.' He made for the front door of the property, beckoning the DS to follow.

Beyond the door frame lines of dark blood were smeared along the white walls. There seemed to be two distinct trails, one slightly higher than the other. They ran thick, initially, heavy in blood, and then thinned into tapered points that looked like digits of a hand. As the detectives stood in the hallway they were joined by DS Phil Donnelly. 'Good to see you, sir.'

Valentine returned the greeting, but it was always odd to have someone say it was good to see you at a murder scene. 'What do you make of this, Phil?'

The detective turned towards the wall, rolled on the balls of his feet. 'Hard to say, looks like two trails.' Donnelly took his hands from his pockets, traced the space between the trails. 'Could be made by one marker, I mean, it's not out of the question.'

'Do we have prints?'

The DS shook his head. 'The duster's on the way, should have them within the hour.'

'Let me know the minute you have them.'

'Yes, sir.'

'If we've got two sets of prints in there then that's two facing murder.'

They stared at the smears on the wall once again. There was no way of separating the two lines, no way of judging if one set was a match in size and shape for the other.

'We need the duster on this right away, Phil.'

'I'll chase him now.' Donnelly tapped his mobile phone, jammed it between ear and shoulder. 'What are you thinking, boss, robbery gone wrong? That would account for the two bods.'

Valentine scanned the interior. 'There's nothing to rob here.'

Donnelly tried to win back some pride. 'Might have been holding something – drugs, drugs money?'

'If you know this is a drugs house, I'd listen to you. Do you know that?'

He shook his head, the phone slipped, he made a clumsy reach to catch it in his hands. 'Shit, that was close.'

Valentine stood waiting for an answer.

'I don't know that much about the place, sir.'

'Then save the conjecture for when we actually know something, son.'

Donnelly wasn't done. 'I was just thinking, from a motive point of view, you know, that if there was cash or drugs here then it would be a good reason to off someone and flee.'

'Yes, of course. And if the crown jewels had been pinched

21

and stashed here, that would be a reason too.' Valentine didn't like sarcasm, in himself or others, but a little humbling on a murder investigation kept everyone alert.

DS Donnelly tried the phone at his ear once again. 'Still ringing.'

Valentine turned towards his detectives. The fey tone was gone; he sounded gruff. 'Let's stick to what we know. I don't want wild conjecture. I don't want guesswork. I want facts and I want an open mind in the absence of those. This is a murder scene not a pub quiz down the local, do you all understand that?'

'Yes, boss.'

'Good.' Valentine knew he had their attention. It would be a stupid member of the squad that tested his seriousness now.

A bell chimed, it was DS McCormack's mobile. 'Emergency just confirmed, sir. The call for police came from the neighbour, Agnes Gilchrist.'

'Good. Maybe she saw something.' The DI cached away the possibilities. 'Right, now that we've got that clear, let's go and take a look at our victim – middle-aged male, white, do we know anything else?'

The detectives stared at the ground.

'C'mon, somebody.'

DS Donnelly turned over his palm where he'd marked the skin with ink. 'The neighbours say the Millars stay here. Sandra Millar's husband died a few years back, she has a daughter called Jade and an older son who doesn't live with them anymore.'

'Ages?'

'Don't know yet. Teenage and twenties on the kids. At a guess, I'd say the mother might be the same as our victim.'

'Do we have a name for him?'

Donnelly scanned his palm again, the pen stood out on his skin under the bright light. 'James Tulloch.'

5

Jade Millar removed her flat palms from her stomach and pulled the sleeves of her jacket over her hands. It was a distraction, to change the course of her thinking, and because *her mother* hated it. She had said it was something four-year-olds did but her mother wasn't there to object. Jade heard her words, though; all day they'd been with her. She didn't know why it should be that today was the first time in her life that she carried around her mother's words.

Who listened to their mother? Who listened to her mother? Fathers were different, she knew girls at school who always did what their father told them because they were too scared not to. She'd been envious of them once. When Dad died she wished that there was someone to tell her what to do. She hated seeing girls dropped off by their fathers at school, taken to the shops, or anywhere at all. It was like they did it just to annoy her.

'Oh, Dad.' Even the word was difficult to say.

Dad was there with her today, too. But that was different, he was always there. She even dreamed about him at night. Alena from school said she never dreamed about her dad and wasn't it a bit strange. 'You should be dreaming about boys, you have Niall for God's sake.'

Alena didn't get it. She always said something annoying;

24

most days Jade ignored her when she had to but not today. Just the thought of Alena's words made her hands form fists.

Jade took out her phone and scrolled down to Alena's name, she paused with her finger over the delete key in her contacts file. She wanted to do it, to get rid of her. It was simple enough to get rid of people, you just deleted their number from your phone and their profile from your Facebook friends list and they didn't exist anymore. Why couldn't the real world be the same?

'Because that's not how the real world works, Jade!' Her mother's words again.

'Go away!' She bashed the side of her head with the phone. 'Go away. Go away.'

She knew she wouldn't go away, though.

'I'll never leave you,' that's what she'd said to her when Dad died. And her mother was tough, her brother had said so, and Darry knew all about being tough. He'd know what to do with this mess.

In the street outside her home a group of people had gathered. Jade watched them from beneath a tree on the other side of the road. There was a police car and an ambulance, another couple of cars with flashing lights that were probably police cars too, and a blue truck that blocked nearly the entire road. Men and women in uniform were taping off the fence, the gate and the bushes. Another group directed the neighbours indoors. It looked like a television show, like the time Brad Pitt had come to Glasgow and it was on the news.

Jade took her hands from the sleeves of her coat, it didn't

seem right to have them there when she knew her mother objected. For a moment she stared at her hands, what should she do with them? God, what was wrong? It was like her mind was missing or all the thoughts had fallen out. She tried her hands in her pockets, felt for her mobile phone and gripped it tightly when she found it.

'Oh, God . . .'

Tears came, slow at first, because they were a surprise to her. But when she knew they were there, rolling down her cheeks, they intensified. They weren't normal tears, they came from another part of her. Tears appeared when you were in pain, she knew all about that, but these were for something else.

She didn't know what to do. Darry said Mum always knew what to do and wouldn't listen to advice that didn't suit her. Jade hadn't said that, they were her brother's words. But wasn't that the problem? She had everything mixed up and Darry wasn't there either, she wished he was.

She couldn't read the message in her phone again, the one she'd sent to her brother at the barracks, because all the words just got jumbled up, started to mean something else. She needed someone to sort out the mess, to tell her everything would be all right.

She pulled up her contacts on the phone again and dialled her brother.

He answered quickly. 'Jade, what's up now?'

She tried to speak but her mouth was numb with all the crying. 'I don't know what to do.'

'What do you mean?' He was still travelling, she could hear noise from the wheels echoing in the cab of the bus.

'Darry, it's Mum. I don't know what to do.'

'What's happened, Jade? Just tell me, slowly.'

'I went home, like you said. I was waiting for you. I . . . I had a fight with Mum and, oh God, Darry I don't know what happened. There's police everywhere, in the house, in the garden. I can't see a thing except police and everyone's out staring at the house.'

'Calm down, Jade. If you get hysterical, it's not going to help you.'

'But I don't know what to do.'

'Where's Mum?'

'I don't know. She was with him. Darry, it's such a mess.' Her sobbing increased.

'You can't go home, Jade. Do you hear me? I don't want you to go near the police. You can't talk to anyone.'

'I'm right across the street, though. And somebody needs to do something.'

Darry exhaled slowly into the phone. 'Jade, you have to listen to me.'

'I know.' The sobbing reached hysteria.

'I'll be in town soon and you can tell me everything but don't talk to anyone before then. I'm staying at Finnie's place, do you remember where that is?'

'I think so.'

Darry's speech quickened. 'Good. It's on the way to the harbour, above the pub. Now, the bloke in the pub is a good lad, his name's Brian and he has the key for Fin's place, you can ask him for it, say you're going to tidy up before your brother arrives.'

'But won't Fin be there?'

27

'He's out of town for a few days. He won't mind you being there because he knows why I'm coming home.'

'You told Fin?'

'I told him some of it, Jade. I had to. He knows I'm not due leave and wouldn't desert the place if it wasn't serious.'

'But . . .'

'Jade, he's an old friend, he understands. He's on our side, honestly.'

'OK.' A tired note played in her voice.

'You sound exhausted, just go now. I'll be home soon.'

'Darry . . .'

'What is it?'

'Promise me everything will be OK.'

'I promise.' His speech stalled, then lit up again. 'Go, Jade, quickly now, and don't stop for anyone.'

Jade held the phone to her ear to make sure her brother had gone. When the line tone changed and the call ended she lowered the phone and stared into the street. Another police car was arriving, she watched the uniformed officers jog towards her house, and she raised the mobile phone again.

'Niall, it's me.'

'Where are you now?'

'I'm at home, I need to see you.'

'OK. Tell me where.'

6

As the corpse appeared in front of him DI Bob Valentine's neck muscles stiffened. It was always the same, like a physical reminder of his calling. He had not joined up to strut about like some of his colleagues, to chase rank. It had been a deeper connection. If he had been looking to attract censure from his father – a striking miner at the time – he could hardly have chosen a worse profession, but that wasn't what he was about. As fathers went, he had a gem; he wouldn't want to injure his pride, or any other part of him. The fact that Valentine signed up for the force had little to do with an intention: the police force took him.

From boyhood the idea of good and evil preoccupied Valentine. Even games like cowboys and Indians or cops and robbers had a deeper, darker edge than with other boys. It seemed, to him, the stuff of life. This was what he was about, he was a hunter and a protector. He had grown up and sworn himself to maintaining the pretence that passed for civil society. He had always known it was written for him. Somewhere was a ledger with the words: *Bob Valentine, finder of sociopaths and psychopaths.*

The wound in James Tulloch's neck drew the detective's interest. Normally, the cause of death would be the first point he looked at but his own stabbing – still so recent – made him recoil. It wasn't the excessive amount of blood, or the torn flesh that protruded above the soaking T-shirt, but the way the sight set his mind tripping back to an unhappy time.

He had tried to seal off the part of his memory that stored the entry of a blade into his chest that punctured his heart. The pain was not what bothered him, or the fifty pints of blood they transfused into him at the hospital; the words 'angiography', 'thoracotomy' and 'heart-lung bypass' were just terms the chief super liked to test his mettle with. He was repaired, almost fully; it was the damage his near death had done to his family, to Clare and the girls, that still worried him.

The kitchen table was nothing special, an old MFI number with a couple of drawers and rickety legs. His late mother would have said it had 'seen better days' but then she would never have had chipboard under her roof in the first place. The sag in the middle, where the weight of a man's torso lay, suggested his mother would be right to assume the product was useless.

Valentine took in the scene, which hinted at surreal domesticity. On the table, beside a spreading pool of blood that threatened to spill over the edge, sat a bottle of HP sauce and a sugar bowl with odd pink splodges inside. There was a packet of Sugar Puffs spread on the floor and some of the contents had been stamped into the linoleum where the blood lay in tacky footprints.

A chip pan on the cooker. A white plastic jug kettle. Fridge. Washing machine. And men in white suits raking the contents of cupboards, drawers and the kitchen counter for whatever they could find.

'No weapon,' said Valentine. It was a statement but everyone at once knew it was also a question that required an answer.

A blue face mask was pulled down. 'No sign of one, sir.'

'What about the cutlery drawer, any knife sets? Steak knives maybe with one missing?'

The mask went back on, head shakes followed.

'Well this is bloody great. A fatal domestic, in the one place of the house you'd expect to find a multitude of weapons and no weapon.'

DS McAlister arrived. 'Not resorting to guesswork are you, boss? Might not have been a domestic.'

'Touché, pal.' He walked round the corpse and peered over the top of the deceased's head. 'It's a tidy scene, too tidy. Maybe a row over the Sugar Puffs – I wouldn't want those for my tea either – and then the knife goes in the back of the neck.'

As Valentine straightened himself the team followed with their eyes. DS McCormack spoke: 'Possibly a panic move, sir. If we go on the assumption most victims know their murderer, and why wouldn't we assume this in a family home, then the sight of him sitting there with a knife in his back would be a shock.'

'So our Bronco Billy retrieves the knife and then . . .' the DI turned around, scanning the floor and down the hall.

'If the assailant's in shock, say it's the woman and this is her partner, she wouldn't want to look.'

'So, she takes off with the knife.'

DS McAlister pointed back to the hall. 'She tanks it, boss, fast as she can. Probably doesn't even realise she's holding the knife, she's in pixie land. There's tears, snot, hysterics.' McAlister waved his hand towards the wall, traced the line of blood smears. 'She's all over the shop, can hardly stand, that's how we get the streaks.'

'Is it?' Valentine's voice indicated a put-down was coming for the theorists. He walked towards Ally. 'Only problem is, son, those smears on the wall, remember, they end in five digits. It's pretty hard to hold a knife, bloody big one at that, with your hands open and pressed to the plasterboard.'

McAlister sucked on his bottom lip. 'So we're talking two people.'

Valentine's eyes widened. 'Could be.'

Valentine strolled round the corpse, keeping his head down and eyes focussed. He appeared to be taking pictures to store in his memory, recording the scene. His breathing stilled and his demeanour became suffused with concentration. When he reached the other side of the corpse he crouched lower beside an outstretched arm, 'Ally, give me that pen.'

'You see something?'

Valentine took the pen and slotted the end under the victim's T-shirt sleeve, pulled back the fabric to reveal more of the arm. A detailed crown and feathers, in faded blue ink, sat beneath the skin. 'Is that military?'

McAlister peered closer. 'A military tattoo – wouldn't we hear drums and pipes, boss?'

'Very funny. Get that snapped and check it out.'

'Will do.'

32

DS Donnelly joined them in the kitchen. 'That's the duster here, sir, I put him on the hall first.'

'Nice one, Phil. And have we had the pleasure of Mr Scott's company?' The fiscal depute had an officious reputation that grated on Valentine. 'Please tell me I haven't missed our regular parley.'

'I'm afraid so, arrived the same time as the doc, so he's been and gone with a death cert in his mitt.'

'Right, in that case, let's get our victim over to pathology. I want whatever secrets he's holding as soon as possible.'

'Yes, boss.'

'And Phil, get uniform to search the grassy patch at the end of the street, and all the way into the town. If the perp took off in a fit of panic chances are the weapon was dumped in a similar fashion.'

DS McAlister spoke: 'Do you want the rest of us back at the station?'

'Not you, you're on the door-to-door with uniform. And remember they're jumpy. We want answers but we don't want anyone upset, do you get me?'

'Yes, sir.'

'Anything at all unusual, I want to know, Ally. If a stray dog took a squirt on the lamppost out there I want it ID'd. Any ructions from the locus, shouting, screaming – get exact times and places. And, Ally, try to get a handle on the type of people we're dealing with. What did the locals think of the Millars and James Tulloch? Where's the teenager? And get a hold of the older kid. When you have a picture, head for the station, make a start pinning what we have on the board.'

The DI headed towards the street, the sky was darkening now. 'Sylvia, get your car, we're going for a jaunt.'

'Yes, sir. Where are we off to?'

'The hospital. Hopefully our witness is compos mentis.'

7

DI Bob Valentine watched the street lamps fizzing into life above the road as they headed out of Whitletts. Darkness hadn't fully arrived yet and the amber glow from above added an unnatural sheen to the route. They had passed the station, and were heading out towards Tam's Brig before Valentine realised they were travelling in the opposite direction of Ayr Hospital.

'Sylvia, I know you've not been in the town long but you should know the hospital's the other way.'

The DS took her gaze from the road. 'She's in Crosshouse, sir.'

'They took her to Kilmarnock when we have that massive hospital here.'

'Better equipped, apparently.'

Valentine tugged at his seatbelt to allow him more room to turn around. 'How bad is this woman? I mean, I don't want to get out there and find out she's in a coma and can't talk.'

'She's stable, I believe. Gave herself a bad knock on the way down, and she's a fair old age, so I'm presuming they're being careful.'

Valentine locked away the information about the victim and how the medics rated the town's main hospital. The place had only been built a few years ago – at least, that's how it looked to him – and now it was outdated compared to the Kilmarnock facility. Everything in the old town was falling apart or closing down. Shops in the centre were being shuttered every other day. Pound stores and charities selling second-hand junk was the only growth area. It didn't feel like a place anyone wanted to live anymore.

'How have you settled in, Sylvia?' he said.

'Well, Ayr's not that far from Glasgow, but it's a long way away if you know what I mean.'

'We'll not be staging the Commonwealth Games here, that's for sure.'

Sylvia accelerated to beat the traffic lights where a junky stood shivering at the pedestrian crossing. 'There are some similarities, though.'

'Junkies you mean. I don't know where they all came from, never saw them until a few years ago . . .' the DI trailed off. 'God, I sound like my father. I'll be blaming Thatcher next.'

The conversation turned briefly to politics, to the state of the country, and then back to the town and their reason for being there.

'We shouldn't complain, sir,' said Sylvia. 'We're probably in the one growth profession.'

'Sad but true. As long as you're not finding the going too tough, I mean, we're not as well resourced as Glasgow out here in the wild west.'

'It's fine. I don't have a life, remember.'

Valentine didn't reply. There was a point among colleagues where day-to-day chat about the job turned into a more personal affair. There had been moments in the past when he had relied on DS McCormack's insights into his personal life but they had always left him feeling compromised, like he owed her something in return. That had been fine when she was merely seconded to Ayr for one specific case but since she had been posted permanently he couldn't take the risk.

As the detectives pulled off the main road, towards Crosshouse Hospital, it became clear that several circuits of the car park would be necessary to find a space. On the way to the entrance the building's bright lights belied the darkness that had crept in. Valentine checked his watch and tried to guess where his wife and family might be now. Chloe's play had finished half an hour ago, they'd all be at Vito's for ice cream, that's what had been planned. The girls loved the ice cream there, no matter how quickly they were growing up that remained constant. He tried to put the picture out of his mind – it wasn't helping anyone – as he approached the reception desk and produced his warrant card. 'DI Valentine and this is my colleague DS McCormack, we're here to see the old lady you brought from Ayr.'

'Oh, yes.'

McCormack said, 'Agnes Gilchrist.'

'Of course.' The receptionist picked up a telephone receiver and waited for an answer, her chat was brisk. 'Doctor's coming to take you through.'

As they sat down Valentine absorbed the familiar setting. Nurses dashing about, the overpowering scent of industrial disinfectant and the occasional chime of medical equipment combined to remind him why he didn't like hospitals. There had been long weeks in such a place, stretching into months, after his own knife assault. At first it was like everything was happening to someone else – like he was a spectator to terrible events – and he indulged the fantasy because it was easier to absorb than the reality that he had died.

Twice on the operating table the detective's heart stopped and he was declared dead. He hadn't fought back, that would have taken a conscious effort, something he didn't have. He was cold, numbed by the drugs, but that was all. There was no retreat from a blinding white light either; God hadn't whispered to him like some Hollywood movie. For a long time afterwards he was too weak, physically and mentally, to do more than ponder what had happened to him. But, later, the questions came.

'Detective Inspector . . .' the man was holding out his hand, 'I'm Dr Campbell.'

'Hello, Dr . . . I'm sorry I was miles away.'

Valentine and McCormack followed the doctor down an over-lit corridor that led to the wards. He was a talkative man, commenting on their shared misfortune to be working so late on a weeknight and the trouble of rising early the next day. When he got to Agnes Gilchrist, however, his tone darkened.

'She's not in a good way, she got a bad knock on the head in the fall. She's an old lady and hasn't kept good health for some time. On top of that we've had to set her wrist, a clean enough break, but she's had an almighty shock.'

'If we can just have a couple of minutes with her,' said Valentine.

'Well that really will be all, I'm afraid. And can I ask you not to let her get worked up, we need to keep her calm and rested.'

'Of course.'

The room was small, dominated by a portable hospital bed that was elevated to allow the patient to sit up. There was a sink, a small wooden cabinet with a plastic water jug and one chair, occupied by an old man in a dark brown suit. The detective was first in the room, followed closely by the others. The old man rose as Valentine passed and the pair nodded to each other. When he reached the side of the bed he stared at the patient and she acknowledged him with a flat smile.

'Hello, Agnes.'

She was nervy, her hands trembling.

'I'm Detective Inspector Valentine and this is DS McCormack.' As the doctor appeared on the other side of the bed Valentine noticed the old man had left the room.

'The police officers would like to ask you a few questions, Mrs Gilchrist.'

Her lips tightened, then parted a little.

'It's OK, love.' Valentine took hold of her hand. 'I know you've been through the mill today, we should be giving you a medal.'

DS McCormack sat on the edge of the bed and asked Agnes if she was comfortable, if they could do anything for her.

'I'm fine, they've been very good to me.'

'Do you mind if we ask a few questions, Mrs Gilchrist?'

'You've got your job to do, son.'

'Can you tell us what you saw?'

'Well, I didn't think much of it at first, it just sounded like another one of their rows with all the shouting and screaming.'

'Who was shouting and screaming?'

'It was herself at first, then her man, I think.'

DS McCormack had been taking notes, she looked up. 'Do you mean Sandra Millar?'

'Yes, I'd know her sobbing anywhere, dogs in the street would know her.'

'You said her man was there too, would that be James Tulloch?'

'I don't know his name. Can't say I've ever had the pleasure.'

'But you recognised him?'

Agnes picked at the hem of the cotton bed sheet with shaking fingers. 'To be honest, I can't say I did. I heard a man, but I don't know who it was.'

'It's OK, Mrs Gilchrist, you're doing fine.'

The old woman looked at the doctor. 'Perhaps that's enough for now,' he said. 'Perhaps after a night's rest she'll remember some more.'

'Just one more question. Did you see, or hear, anyone else?'

'I . . . I just can't be sure. Is that important?'

'Think hard for a moment, I know you're tired, but this would be a great help.' Valentine's voice trailed into stillness as he tried to comfort the old woman. 'Was Sandra Millar's daughter there, or her son? What about somebody else altogether?'

Agnes drew a deep breath and passed her gaze between

the detective and the doctor. The task that had been asked of her was too much for her exhausted state.

'I really think we should leave it there,' said Dr Campbell.

'There were two people.'

'Go on,' the DI whispered to her.

'When I called the police someone had staggered out the house but she was already sitting on the front step screaming and crying. I did see two people, a man and a woman, one was definitely bigger.'

'You saw a man?'

'Yes, I saw him coming from the house and going down the street. And it couldn't have been her man because he was . . .' Agnes's eyes were moistening, her voice croaking and cracking, 'he was in the kitchen.'

The doctor stood up, frowning, and directed an open hand towards the door. Valentine and McCormack followed his lead.

'Thank you, Agnes. You've been a tremendous help to us.' Valentine was sure the witness had more to reveal about her neighbour's death but it was impossible to push her further in her current condition. 'If you remember anything else please pick up the phone. Tomorrow we'll pay you another little visit when you've had some rest.'

In the corridor Valentine tried to make sense of the new information but he knew it only raised more questions. If she had recognised the man, or been able to identify someone, then that would have been helpful. As it was, all the DI now had was another suspect to add to the list.

DS McCormack was putting away her notebook and zipping up her bag as the DI met her at the door. Her expression indicated that she had already moved beyond the significance of the witness statement.

'Sir, can I ask just one question?'

'Sure. Fire away.'

'Who the hell were you nodding to when you went in the room?'

Valentine didn't reply.

8

On the road back to Ayr Valentine tapped the window sill with his fingertips and waited for DS McCormack to begin her cross-examination. It was something she did well, not in the professional sense, but through her ability to make others reveal secrets they might prefer to keep to themselves. Valentine's mother had been the same, his father had called her an *accomplished ear lender* for her skill in making others talk their problems away to her. He envied that of his father – how much easier would his own life be with a wife more like his mother? It was nonsense, of course. He was married to Clare, she had supported him in more ways than he was able to tally, and she had given him the girls – the true wonder of his life.

'I know what you're thinking,' he said.

'You do?'

Valentine pulled his hand away from the window. 'You think I'm hiding something, like I did on the Janie Cooper case.'

Some cases were repeated in conversation among officers and others were stoppered in the past. The missing schoolgirl was one of those cases that no one mentioned. Until now, the DI and the DS had never even tried to talk about it.

'Oh, we're back there are we?' said McCormack.

'I'd sooner not be.'

'Am I to assume that you're there whether you want to be or not?'

'I don't know.'

'OK. That tells me all I need to know. How long have you felt like this?'

'I never said I felt like anything, Sylvia.'

'You didn't need to. It's burning out of you, and yes, like it was on the Cooper case.'

Valentine reached for the window button, let some air in. 'It's hot in here.'

'I know what that case did to you, Bob. I saw it, you let it get out of hand and I told you that at the time. If you're in the same place again, you need to do something about it.'

The detective nearly laughed, but produced a guttural throat clearing. 'Right . . .'

It had started with nightmares on the Cooper case. Sweat-soaked nights when he would wake trembling and vaguely terrified from the sight of something he couldn't explain. It didn't feel like a dream, more a glimpse of a time or place that existed elsewhere. He had put it down to his temperament – this was his first case after the stabbing – he didn't know how to adjust to life again. He was weakened, in body and spirit, unsure of who he was. But the nightmares were just his resting mind playing this out, surely. And then they started to appear in the waking world.

'And what would you recommend I do, ask the chief super to reinstate my visits to the shrink?' said Valentine.

'No. I don't think a police psychologist is remotely qualified to deal with your problem, sir.'

Now he did laugh, though he found nothing she said funny. 'It would be the psychologist with the heart problems by the end of it.'

Valentine hadn't told DS McCormack that the nightmares and visions from the Cooper case had never ended. He tried to get used to them, let them become a part of his new reality in the hope that they would stop. But they never did. He learnt to live with the occasional unease that he wasn't quite as firmly settled in the real world as others but his heightened senses made this difficult.

'What happened back there at the hospital?' said McCormack.

Even though he knew the question was coming it still jolted him. 'I don't know.'

'Oh, come on. I saw your face.'

There was no point in misleading the DS, she had experience of dealing with people in Valentine's situation from past cases. Any of the others on the squad, or even Clare, wouldn't know what to say and would judge him accordingly. But McCormack was different.

'OK. I saw a man,' said Valentine.

'What? In the room?'

'In the room with us. A little old man, in a brown tweed suit.'

'And you didn't think that was strange?'

'I thought it was Mrs Gilchrist's husband at first.'

'At first?'

45

'Yes. I saw him sitting there, he got up, nodded to me and then when I looked again he was gone.'

DS McCormack held the wheel straight as the car crossed yellow chevrons leading up to the roundabout. She passed an open junction and accelerated beyond a grey saloon before speaking again. 'I knew it.'

'Knew what?'

'When we had the parapsychologist in Glasgow, that time I told you about with the missing persons, I got quite taken with the whole subject, kind of immersed myself in it.'

'You said.'

'Well, the psychic told me that when people are dying, or about to die, preparing to die, that's when the passed souls gather. The spirits of those they once knew surround them.'

The suggestion unsettled Valentine; it wasn't an explanation he wanted to believe in. 'You see, this is just the kind of thing I have trouble with, Sylvia.'

'I don't understand.'

'No. Neither do I. That's exactly it. I don't buy into it because this is precisely the kind of thing that any old crank can make up.'

She pinched her cheeks, her reply came with a flat delivery. 'You mean because it's not taken from a textbook or a manual it's irrelevant. I know what you mean, I had that problem too but you need to realise this isn't car maintenance or police procedure, all you know goes right out the door. It's what you feel that matters.' She glanced sideways. 'What do you feel, Bob?'

'Honestly? I feel like I'm being messed with.'

46

'Well, welcome to my world. We all feel like that.'

'Not in this way. I need to be on my game, this is a murder hunt, Sylvia. I can't collate the facts surrounding the taking of a life when I don't know what's real and what's not.'

They'd reached the turn-off for Ayr. The blinkers flashed on the wet tarmac as the car decelerated. 'I think I know a way to help. If you'll let me.'

The offer was made once before and Valentine rejected it. This time, however, he knew there may not be another offer. The Cooper case still lingered in memory too, he couldn't go through another bout like that. If it was happening again, he needed to do something. There was no running away, ignoring it wasn't possible and the clumsy approach he'd adopted the last time nearly killed him. So was he scared? Yes, but not to face it, only to accept it because that meant it was real.

'I don't know, Sylvia. I have to think about this.'

'OK, but don't take too long. Thinking's rarely the answer, Bob. Someone once told me that.'

9

DI Bob Valentine sat in his car on the edge of Barns Street and watched DS McCormack begin a three-point turn in the road. It was a wide street, one of Ayr's more expansive Georgian terraces that had once been filled with comfortable family homes, but was now replaced by dentist surgeries, lawyers' offices and the occasional surveyors. The DS struggled with the simple manoeuvre and eventually stopped with the car blocking one side of the road. Was she all right? For a moment Valentine contemplated going over, then he noticed her lips moving and knew she must have taken a call. It was brief, and when she was finished the reverse lights lit up.

The DI was lowering his window as she drew up next to him. 'What's up, Sylvia?'

'That was Ally, the station just took a call from Crosshouse.'

Before she relayed the news Valentine already guessed what it must be. 'Agnes Gilchrist?'

'She just passed away.'

He hit the heel of his hand off the steering wheel. 'Damn it.'

'I'm sure her family's less than pleased, too.'

'I'm sorry. I didn't mean it to come out like that.'

'I know.' McCormack put her car in gear; it was late, time to be home. 'She's in safe hands now, Bob.'

Valentine lifted his gaze in time to see the knowing frown on the DS's face as she drove off. 'Passed souls gather round a deathbed, eh, Sylvia.' He was sure McCormack would have more to say on the matter. She would only mention the subject again when he was ready, though. It was up to him if he wanted to accept her offer of help. That he needed help was hardly under question, but accepting there was even an issue would have to be surmounted first.

On the way to Masonhill the detective's thoughts turned to his arrival in the family home. The knowledge that he had missed his daughter's stage debut coincided with an irritation in the lining of his gut. Too much vending-machine coffee? The pre-packaged sandwiches? It might have been either but he suspected the reflux was psychosomatic.

It was late, the girls would be in bed. Clare was likely to be in her bed too, but she wouldn't be asleep. She didn't sleep when he was working late. She propped herself up on cushions, a book on show but not being read, and rehearsed her recriminations.

As Valentine pulled into the drive he noticed a light burning in the new extension. For years Clare had campaigned for extra space but it had taken his father's decline in health to turn the wish to a necessity. Four months had passed since the building work finished but the DI still wasn't sure he had done the right thing. Clare was happy to have a bigger home, had delighted in being able to match their neighbours for once, but the place had changed.

The combination of having his father home and the girls growing up made Clare introspective and it worried Valentine.

The hallway sat in darkness, only a little light seeping through from the kitchen at the back of the house. He was used to coming home to silence, of having to remove his shoes so as not to wake the girls and to give Clare a chance to go to sleep now he was home. He followed the light to the kitchen and on to his father's room where he tapped the door frame.

'Hello, Dad.'

'Oh, hello. I thought you were on an all-nighter.'

'No. Done as much as I can.'

His father sat in front of him with a cup of tea. 'Kettle's still warm, want a drink?'

'No, I'm OK.' He moved into the room, pulled out a chair. 'How was Chloe?'

'She was amazing!' His father's heavy eyes widened as he spoke.

'Really, she was that good?'

'Oh, yes. A star is born.' He picked up his cup, plugged his mouth. When he spoke again, the subject had changed. 'It must have been serious them dragging you away like that.'

'About as serious as it gets.'

'I don't know what this town is coming to, I'm just glad your mother isn't around to see it. Mind you, it's the girls I worry about.' He raised the cup again.

'How was Clare, you know, about me leaving in a hurry?'

'She was fine.'

'I doubt that, Dad.'

'Well, she gets a little worked up now and again, but it's just because she cares. She wants the family together, wants you to see more of the girls, you can't blame her for that.'

'No. I can't blame her for that.'

Since he had moved in, his father had become like a resident counsellor, listening to everyone's concerns and making sure each party considered them. Valentine didn't object because his father had already saved his marriage once and he hoped the experience might confer some wisdom on him. There were times when so many competing challenges assailed his mind that clear thought became impossible. The job took priority and family suffered, most of the time. His father would never get into that situation, and he envied and admired that.

'Still, who am I to tell you how to run your life? I'm just a house guest.'

'You're family, Dad.'

'No. Clare and the girls are your family.'

'Don't let Clare hear you say that, her days revolve around getting the lot of us to sit down to dinner together.'

'She's a nest builder.'

The term lodged itself with his current thoughts, it wasn't welcome, made him think he might be the very opposite. By looking out for other families, had he neglected his own? Surely a father's priorities should stop at his front door, didn't everyone else's? 'I really should get to bed now.'

'You get some sleep, son.'

51

Clare turned the light out and faced the wall as Valentine entered the bedroom. He undressed in the dark, as noiselessly as possible, though not without stubbing a toe on the dresser.

'Christ above.'

'You'll wake the house,' said Clare.

'What if I've broken my toe?'

'You'll be driving yourself to hospital.'

He sat on the bed, rubbing his toe. 'I'm just back from there.'

'What?' Clare turned round.

'Not for me, for work.'

'Oh, I see.'

'I didn't mean to give you a fright.'

'You mean you don't want me to worry about you. My husband with his damaged heart, who nearly died on the job, who leaves his family to run to the latest crime scene.'

Valentine reclined on the bed. 'We've spoke about this, Clare. I have a job to do.'

'You have a family too.'

There was no point in arguing with her, the conversation had been covered before. The only reply Clare wanted to hear was one that he could not give her. Not now the girls were heading for university and his father was living with them in an expensive new extension. 'A man died tonight. And an old lady. They had family too.'

'Not your family.'

'Have you any idea how cold that sounds?'

Clare spun round and pulled the light on. 'Don't give me that, Bob. I'm not going to listen to the public service broadcast anymore. It's all very sad that we live in a world where people are running around killing each other but there is nothing I can do about that and very little that you or anyone else can. You have a family, a wife, two beautiful daughters who worship you, and an elderly father who won't be around for ever. It's about time you started devoting some of your precious time – and I mean precious, you are not well enough for this either – to your own people. You need to understand that because if you don't then your next shock might be the last.'

The light went out and Clare moved to her side of the bed.

Valentine didn't consider a reply because there was nothing he could say that hadn't already been said. When he came home with a blue folder under his arm, his first day of active policing after the stabbing, she cried. Just seeing that small oblong of cardboard meant days filled with worry and nights without sleep when she didn't know if her husband was alive or dead.

He didn't want to hurt Clare but what choice did he have? There was only one way to conduct a murder investigation and that was by devoting himself to it. He couldn't leave the station and forget about the case. Two people had died now. They deserved better.

As he closed his eyes and tried for sleep the detective pressed the thick ridge of flesh in the centre of his chest. The scar tissue was hard, a bulging seam that marked the point where death had touched him. So much had changed since that day, he had questioned everything about his life, but he had resolved nothing. Clare was right, the time for answers was coming.

10

Darren Millar's journey from the east coast to the west was filled with panic. Since fleeing Glencorse Barracks, without permission, he expected to be identified every time he turned onto a new street. People were staring, hostile. To avoid scrutiny he waited outside Penicuik bus station in the rain, rather than under the sheltered roof of the depot. His nervousness peaked when he joined the queue on the concourse but as the bus finally departed he got a fleeting sense of freedom. The delusion was soon replaced by serious nervousness as the journey progressed. Stomach cramps and incessant worry arrived. This wasn't the same as the early panic that he might get caught, and returned to barracks for a kicking, but a sustained and terrible fear his family wouldn't survive without him.

Jade was always a worry, but weren't all little sisters like that? He expected his friend Finnie to look out for her, to make sure she went to school and didn't stay out all night, but that clearly hadn't been happening. He wouldn't be escaping barracks and rushing home, or fielding phone calls and text messages from Jade – some into the wee hours – if everything was OK.

His mother had said that Jade needed help. She was too young to understand what losing Dad meant at the time, but as she got older the realisation that she no longer had a father was always going to cause problems. 'Being a teenager was hard enough,' Mum said at the time and Darren knew she was right.

They were so cruel, kids. After the funeral he'd taken a few days off school, everyone knew though. They'd had time to talk, to identify a change in him. On the first day back in woodwork he went through the tasks slowly, silently. They watched him, hoping to see some indication of the change but when none came a prompt appeared.

'Hey, Darry . . .' said Kevin Houston. He wasn't one of the bigger lads, but the most brash and ignorant. He smiled for the other boys, raised his voice a little. 'What are you making with that wood – it's not a coffin is it?'

The whole class laughed. Houston grinned as the boys jeered, he'd said the words but it might have been any of them. They all scented weakness, every one was attacking.

'I'll have you for that,' said Darren. But even as he said it he knew he didn't have the heart, it would mean tackling the whole class.

As the bus pulled in to the station at Ayr, Darren Millar wiped away the moisture on the inside of the windowpane. It was dry outside now, but the earlier rain that was brought in on coats and umbrellas still clung to the congested bodies. He hadn't expected the scene to be so prosaic, the streets so familiar and the people so unaware of the importance of his arrival. He didn't know what he expected, really. Everything was so instinctual, the call for help, the flight. Did it even matter what happened next? Not to him.

Certainly not for him, because he wasn't there for himself. None of this was about him.

Darren checked his mobile phone as he left the bus – there were no messages from Jade. If she'd had any trouble finding Finnie's flat she would have called. She always had the phone in her hand, or at least within reach. Lately, it was like she had his number on speed dial, like she didn't want to be away from the sound of his voice for too long. It was another pressure to add to all the rest. They needed to have a talk, she needed to know that there were times when her brother would be there for her and there were times when it was simply impossible. If he could make her see that, then the visit home might be worth all the trouble.

On the way to the flat, Darren passed the Meat Hangers nightclub where Finnie worked. It was closed up, the front window had been covered with a large square of plywood like it had been smashed and a replacement hadn't arrived yet. He edged up to the front door and tried to see inside but it was too dark. There were no lights on, nobody there. He didn't expect to see Finnie, he'd said that he wasn't going to be around, but he hadn't said anything about the club closing, which he found strange.

At Finnie's flat Darren eyed the smokers outside the pub. They were typical Ayr types. Teenage girls in short, tight dresses. A pot-bellied taxi driver looking for a fare. A man with raw features, reddened from heavy drinking, using the wall for support. Darren might have been away for a century, the place wouldn't change. He could arrange the interchangeable scenes from memory, it was depressingly familiar.

In the doorway the handle was moving downwards as he arrived.

'Who the hell are you?' The man's face stayed firm as he spoke, for a moment he eyeballed Darren like he was sizing up his threat, and then he pivoted back towards the door and held it open for another, bigger man.

'What's it to do with you?' said Darren.

'Don't get lippy with me, son.' He stepped forward to allow the second man space in the doorway. 'And I'll ask the questions. So, come on, who are you?'

'I'm Darren Millar.'

His expression said the name didn't mean anything.

The bigger man spoke. 'He's Finnie's army pal.'

'So you know him. Where is he?'

Darren edged onto the street. 'How should I know? I'm not his keeper.'

'But you were about to chap his door.'

'I was. Doesn't mean I can see through wood, does it?'

'I've warned you about that lip already. You'll have trouble talking at all with a mouth the shape of Joe's fist.'

The two men followed Darren into the street, the smokers outside the pub looked on, eager for the possibility of entertainment. As he stepped away Darren looked up towards the window of the flat. 'What were the pair of you doing up there?'

'Just a social call.'

Darren started to nod. 'Fin still work for you?'

'How do you know that?'

'You're Norrie Leask. I was just at your place, it's all boarded up.'

Leask's eyes narrowed as his heavy brows pressed down. 'You're either very smart, or very stupid, pal. Either way, you're lucky I don't have the time for this tonight. But you tell your friend I want a word with him, and yesterday's too soon. Got that?'

Darren didn't reply. He watched Leask and the man called Joe walk towards a car on the other side of the road. They exchanged words over the roof before getting inside and chatting some more; Leask seemed to be giving directions on the road ahead. Darren waited for them to drive away and then went inside. As he opened the door the flat was in darkness, completely still.

'Jade . . .'

There was no answer.

'Jade, where are you?'

Movement. The sound of more than one body.

'No. Don't hurt him!' Jade's voice edged into a scream.

As Darren turned on the light he had to drop to the floor to avoid a cricket bat that was swinging towards his head.

'Jesus.'

A loud thud on the wall was followed by a small cloud of plaster. Darren got to his feet, fists drawn, and started hooking punches before his attacker had time to respond.

'No. Stop.'

Jade squeezed herself between her brother and the target of his fists.

'Stop!'

Darren stepped back, he was breathing heavily.

'Start explaining, Jade, I mean it. I want to know what's going on now.'

11

Detective Inspector Bob Valentine didn't think he would miss the old Saltmarket mortuary but so many pieces of his personal history had disappeared that he now found himself feeling nostalgic for the place. It had been too small for its purpose, the technicians always moaned about negotiating the steps with coffins or wheeled stretchers, but it was big enough to hold his memories. As he drove towards the new morgue at the Southern General, the DI replayed his first visit to the place.

'Penny for them,' said DS McCormack.

'You wouldn't thank me for my thoughts right now.'

'Oh right, like that is it?'

Valentine turned down the radio, gripped the steering wheel. 'Well, if you must know I was thinking about the early days, when I was green as grass, and made those scary, first trips to the morgue.'

'The wee one at the High Court, where they had the Bible John victims?'

'And Peter Manuel's victims as well.'

'It was a funny place, so unassuming. Didn't look like it was a place chock-full of death.' She stretched out her neck, trying to catch a look at the detective. 'Come on then, what ghoulish pranks did they play on you?'

'There was nothing like that. I just remember watching everyone carrying on like there was no death in the room. You could smoke in those days, they'd pass fags about and chat about the football results or what had just been on the telly. Nobody was bothered about the half-naked dead folk lying around. It shocked me, but you get used to it, don't you?'

McCormack nodded. 'Do you remember the very first time you saw a dead body?'

'Aye, a jumper in the Clyde. He was white as a sheet, apart from the black veins under the skin.'

'Mine was actually at the old morgue. I think they were winding me up because they thought I was a daft wee lassie. I got the tour and then they asked me if I wanted to see some dead folk. I didn't, of course, but I couldn't let on and have them laugh at me.'

'So you said yes?'

'Of course. The first drawer they pulled out was OK, it was an old woman who'd collapsed during a burglary, she just looked tired, worn out. I wasn't fazed but that was my biggest mistake, they started to up the ante then. I saw a few more on slabs and then they took me through to a special room, with a dozen corpses under white sheets.' She shut her eyes tight at the memory.

'Go on, you can't stop there.'

'The first one was a throat slashing that had been closed with clips, it looked like something out of Hammer horror. Then there was a road smash that needed cutting out, there was nothing recognisable as a human being at all, I could only tell one end from the other by the patch of black hair.

I was just about managing to keep my breakfast down at this stage and then they showed me a wee boy who had been hanged on a tree by his satchel strap. He was cold, chalk white like your Clyde jumper. I think I could handle the grizzly stuff but the wee boy's face was so calm and they'd straightened his tie, parted his hair. I ran out of there in floods of tears.'

Valentine listened to the end of her story and empathised. 'The little kiddies are the ones that really get to you.'

'Like Janie Cooper, you mean?'

He didn't respond. The exit for the Southern was yards ahead. He flicked on the indicator.

As they parked, McCormack spoke again. 'Look, I'm sorry. I don't mean to pressure you.'

'It's all right, Sylvia.'

'I'm only trying to help.'

'I know.'

'I'll shut up now.'

'You better had, we have a job of work to attend to.' He locked the car and headed for the mortuary.

The pathology technician directed the detectives to the over-lit room where they had lain out the victim's body. A large inverted Y-shape marked where the main incisions had been made. He was a large man, broad-shouldered and deep-chested. His neck and arms were heavily muscled and despite his fifty-plus years he had clearly been in good condition. As Valentine's gaze took in the man's dimensions he questioned if they had the correct corpse.

'Are we sure this is our man, he looks huge?' he said.

'It's definitely him, look at the tattoo, sir.'

As McCormack spoke the pathologist entered the room, struggling to fit a pale blue gown over his head. 'The Royal Highland Fusiliers, if I'm not mistaken,' he said.

'I thought it was military,' said Valentine. 'And hello to you too, Wrighty.'

'Good morning to you both.' He struggled to fasten the gown behind his back. 'My old man was a bit of a militaria buff, I recognise the crown formation.'

'Well you've saved Sylvia a trip to Google, I'm sure she'll thank you later.'

The detectives collected polythene folders from the technician. Inside was the pathology report, printed on white A4 paper.

'We have ID'd him,' said Valentine, he turned to McCormack.'

'Yes. His name's James Tulloch, he was fifty-four.'

'We took him in for assaulting a previous partner in the nineties and never saw him again so our details are a bit sketchy. Phil and Ally are profiling his latter years now.'

The pathologist looked at the clock. 'Right, there's one or two aspects I'd like to point out if you don't mind cracking on. I've got a bloody appointment at Specsavers in half an hour.'

The DI motioned to the corpse with an open hand. 'Fire away. We're all busy people.'

'Well, just follow on the notes and I'll go through the main points.' He pushed between the fingers of his gloves and walked towards the slab.

Valentine flipped pages. 'He looked much smaller at the scene.'

'A trick of perspective no doubt. If he was crouched over, shoulders facing forward, that would diminish his bulk. A fit and healthy man, though.'

The DI read through the notes on Tulloch's cardiovascular system, it had become a habit with him. There were no congenital abnormalities, no evidence of fibrosis or inflammation. The report said all coronary segments and arteries were normally distributed and only a minimal atherosclerosis was noted. But, just how would his own post-mortem look by comparison?

'The bladder wall was intact and the urine clear. We never found anything to raise suspicions there.'

Valentine tapped the page. 'The stomach contents were clear too.'

'Mainly unidentifiable, almost fully digested.'

'There goes my Sugar Puffs theory.'

Wrighty put his fingertips on the rim of the slab and frowned. 'I'm not even going to ask. Do you want to hear the interesting bits?'

'Go on.'

'The cause of death was undoubtedly the neck trauma, in particular the severing of the spinal column. The wound track, back to front, was administered on a horizontal thrust – that's interesting, don't you think?'

'It is if you say it is, perhaps you can elaborate.'

'Are you up on your bull fighting, Bob?'

'Not the last time I looked.'

'In bull fighting circles this type of wound is known as

the *coup de grâce*. It's how they dispatch the bull, put it out of its misery quickly.'

'Are you saying I should be looking for a matador?' the group shared a laugh. 'Or that this was a professional killing?' Valentine knew the pathologist couldn't answer the question, but it was interesting to watch his reaction.

'Oh, come on, you know that's above my pay grade.'

'That puts it well above mine then.'

'The wound was inflicted by someone who knew how to locate the spinal chord, that's as far as I can surmise, Bob.'

McCormack looked up from her folder. 'It says here there was a head injury too.'

'I was just getting to that. I did find an irregular scalp and skull defect near the midline of the occipital region.'

'In English, Wrighty.'

'Someone bumped him on the back of the head, with something heavy. No idea what, before you ask, I couldn't find any metallic, wood or any other fragments so your guess is as good as mine.'

Valentine folded his report and tucked it inside his jacket. His gaze fell on the deceased but he was addressing the room as he spoke. 'Someone whacked him on the head, enough to knock him out but not to kill him.' He looked to the pathologist for confirmation.

'It's a significant head wound, I'm sure it would have rendered even a fit man like this unconscious.'

'So he's knocked out, but still with us when the *coup de grâce* is administered to finish the job?'

'That's about the strength of it.'

'Well, I find that very interesting.'

'Very.' He waved in the technician. 'Now the difficult work begins.'

'It does indeed.'

12

Chief Superintendent Marion Martin stood in front of a filing cabinet with the top drawer open, peering into a blue folder. She scratched at the corner of her mouth with a long fingernail as her eyes moved back and forth over the printed page. With her tight black skirt, and the small white collar of her blouse pointing to the ceiling, it seemed like a pose she had practised, or perhaps stolen from a magazine.

As Valentine entered he asked himself how long the CS might stand with her back to him before acknowledging he was there. He knew the answer was *as long as she liked* so he stationed himself in the seat in front of her desk. He stared out the window that dominated one wall of the large office. The town of Ayr, pelted by rain, looked grey and bleak beyond the blurry splatter marks and failed to hold his attention. As he turned back to the CS he willed her to break concentration, but when that became a bore he tried noisy throat clearing.

'I hear you, Bob,' said CS Martin.

'If I've come at a bad time, I can try again later.' He eased himself out of the chair; he was too busy to play witness to her display of power.

'Sit.'

A cheeky response came to him: *Is there a dog in the room?* But he suppressed it, did as he was told and retreated into the seat.

'Right, Bob. Tell me about this team-building exercise.' She yanked her chair out and positioned herself precariously on the edge, facing the DI over linked fingers.

Had he heard her properly? Surely she wasn't going to bring up the paintball or the go-karts again. There was a murder investigation under way. A man had been brutally killed the night before. And a few hours before that there had been a robbery with aggravated assault. No one at the station was short of things to do.

'I'm sorry, at the risk of sounding daft, could you repeat that please?'

'I think you heard me.'

The chair was uncomfortable, too hard to sit in. Valentine eased himself onto his elbows and tried to redistribute his weight. 'Is that why you called me in here, boss?'

'Well it wasn't to enquire about your health, Bob.'

There had been a time when she had been very interested in enquiring about his health. After the stabbing, when she had packed him off to look after stripling recruits at the Tulliallan training college, she seemed very keen to know how soon he could return to her murder squad. That was, it seemed, the extent of her interest in her colleagues. She asked after their well-being only when there was a possible threat to her rotas and the station's clean-up rate.

When he returned to the squad Martin had been horrified at the amount of damage to his heart, at the blood loss and the fifty-plus pints that had been transfused into his body.

She said she had seen less horrific post-mortem reports. She did not, however, ask how Clare and the girls were dealing with the situation. The idea that she should ask her own DI how he was didn't occur to her either.

Valentine didn't interpret Martin's comments in a personal manner, but weighed them against the demands of her job. She didn't care how individuals felt or coped, or how high the case files were stacked. Her interest was in getting the job done in the most efficient manner, making sure the paperwork was completed properly, everything else was an irrelevance.

'The team-building exercise is not one of my priorities right now, I'm afraid,' said Valentine.

She dropped her chin onto her chest. 'Well you better bloody make it a priority because I have a presentation to make to the divi' commander a week on Wednesday that should include some pictures of smiling DCs and at least one DI in some form of fancy dress, am I making myself clear?'

'I think I see where you're coming from.'

'Good, Bob. Don't let me down or I'll kick your balls so hard you'll be shaving pubes off your neck.'

'Was that everything?'

'No, I want you to tell me how you're getting on with this killing out at Whitletts.'

He detailed the murder scene for her, summarised the victim's previous conviction for assaulting a former partner and revealed what limited background reports had been passed on. When he was finished, Valentine expected her to ask for written confirmation, but she rose and walked to the corner of the room where a coffee maker sat on top of a two-drawer filing cabinet.

'What the hell is happening to this town? Ayr used to be a nice place to grow up, to go to work and raise your children. Every day I hear more bloody horror stories, it makes you want to pack up and leave them to it.' She poured a coffee, turned back to her desk. 'I'd offer you one but you're just leaving and I'm all out of biccies.'

The DI wished she was serious about packing up. 'Some of us don't have that many options.'

She caught him in her gaze as she sat down again; his remark didn't seem to merit a response. 'And what about the partner, where's she?'

'Sandra Millar's not been seen since last night.'

'The old woman spotted her, the one that passed away.'

'That's right, Agnes Gilchrist saw her fleeing the murder scene. She also saw an unidentified man. And then there's the daughter, Jade, and the son, Darren. Both missing. I'm just about to check with the team what the door-to-door turned up last night but experience tells me this isn't your usual domestic gone wrong.'

'What do you mean by that, Bob?'

Valentine looked to the floor, his foot was making a stiff angle to his ankle. 'Something about the scene, that kitchen was untouched and there was no indication of a struggle. This isn't a classic case of poverty breeding violence, if it was we'd have seen some evidence of that.'

Martin pressed herself further into her chair, the distracted look was gone. Her focus was on the case, on her DI's words. 'Maybe there had been violence previously.

Maybe there had been so much violence that there was no need for a trigger incident.'

'Possibly.'

'Of course, that would make it premeditated.'

'And entirely outside the norm for this sort of thing. Look, what we do have on our side is that, either way, Tulloch most likely knew his killer. We might even get lucky and find the killer was very close to home.'

'We need to find that murder weapon, as soon as possible.' The mention of the knife almost prompted him to mention the pathologist's remark about the precision cutting of the spinal column, but he knew not to overload the chief super. If he gave her too much information she would only use it to hinder him. She liked to see simple solutions to every case but Valentine knew that rarely happened. He held back, it was in the post-mortem report anyway, she could find it for herself.

Valentine rose from the chair. 'Murder weapon or partner. Right now I'd settle for one or the other.'

'Go and see what Ally and Phil turned up. And keep me in the loop.'

'Will do.'

Her voice lifted. 'And I mean it, Bob. Don't dismiss the fact that this case might be a violent domestic that got out of hand, try and rule that out before you go chasing rainbows.'

'Well that would make for a quicker clean-up, for sure.'

'That's not what I'm getting at. I'm on about prioritising.'

He reached for the door handle. 'I'll bear that in mind, boss. That and the team-building exercise.'

13

DI Bob Valentine learned early in his working life that there was nothing noble in toadying to people like CS Martin. There was nothing to be gained by those who toadied to him either, and they often found their actions had the opposite of their desired effect. He was not so blunt as to come down on the side of the plain speaker – the blurt whatever you like brigade – he reserved another kind of disdain for them. And by this point, he had seen them all, or as the Scots said 'met yer type afore'.

People were simple when you got beyond the fronts of respectability, personality and bluster. Confronted, and he was a man who liked to confront, their base motives were the same. People were selfish, composed of egocentric desires and petty envies that often tugged at their ideas of worth. Few were aware enough to understand their own desires or cared to look beyond the task of satisfying their needs.

Noting the universal cues that people showed was a depressing exercise for Valentine. He made decisions about people quickly and never altered them. Those he regarded as opponents became non-existent to him. He isolated them in company, ignored them in private and treated them with indifference when fate brought them together. It was not arrogance on his part, but a deep weariness that cancelled out his usual humanity for his fellow man. When he examined this trait of compartmentalising people, he understood it as a simplified way of separating the good and evil in people. He didn't want to look too closely, however, because one might be more prevalent than the other, and his life was about keeping the two apart.

The DI's thoughts were interrupted by a familiar voice.

'Hello, Bob,' said DI Harris.

'Eddy, nearly walked by you there, in a world of my own.'

DI Eddy Harris fitted the stereotype of the Ayrshire big man perfectly. It was a generic trait, usually passed on by fathers soured by life's injustices. You could pick out the Flash Harrises on the force by their strut and the seething, sneering looks they reserved for those in uniform or of a lower rank. It was a generational hand-me-down that should have died out by now, but plenty of men like Harris still perpetrated chauvinism as a right.

'I'm on my way to see Dino, presume you're on your way out?' said Harris.

'That's right. And delighted about it.'

'Christ, I knew I should have got her a bag of Bonios.'

'Tranquilliser dart might be more appropriate.' Valentine didn't want to be reminded of the chief super, he eased the conversation in another direction. 'How's the club raid, Meat Hangers wasn't it?'

'Little or nothing to go on so far. Waiting for the SOCOs' report but looking too clean for my liking, not a shred to go on.'

'It's one of Norrie Leask's joints isn't it? That should be your starter for ten.'

'If the report comes back full of holes, Leask'll get a good rattle, don't worry about that.' DI Harris headed for the chief super's office, waving off his colleague as he went.

As Valentine opened the door of the incident room he watched the heads turn, but the gazes aimed on him were jerked away. Eyes met computer screens, the surface of desks, the interior of drawers. No one waited to meet his returned stare, except DS McCormack. She stood with a blue folder pressed to her hip and an unreadable expression on her face. For a moment, the DI tried to discern the look, relate it to some stock image he carried in his head but as the seconds passed a creeping self-consciousness diverted him. He pressed forward, headed for the incident board at the far end of the long room.

'Hello, boss,' said DS McAlister.

'Ally . . .'

'Any good news to report?'

'That depends. How optimistic are you feeling?'

As Valentine reached the board he put his hands in his pockets and stood before the team's input. There were pictures now, from the crime scene and from the police files. The murder victim, crouched over a blood-daubed kitchen table, held the most prominent position, flanked by a dated-looking mug shot of James Tulloch and smaller, insignificant-looking photographs of a young man in uniform.

The DI pointed. 'This the brother?'

'Yes, sir. That's Darren Millar, aka Darry the lad, aka Corporal Millar of the . . .'

'He's still military?'

'Very much so. And get this, they're as stumped as us as to his whereabouts.'

'You mean he's AWOL?'

'Too right he is. Posh bloke at the barracks was very cagey, not giving much away, but you could tell they're spewing about it.'

'They tend to take a dim view of squaddies on the run.'

'Yeah. He wants a word, by the way.'

'Who, Ally?'

'Forgot his name, Major Misunderstanding or something. There's a Post-it on your desk with his details but I got the impression he'd be calling back before you got to him.'

DS Donnelly and DS McCormack joined the others at the incident board. It seemed a good time for Valentine to summon the rest of the room to gather around. The sound of chairs scraping and footsteps followed.

'OK, we know what we're looking at here, murder is not something we ever approach in the low gears, so I want your full attention and your full commitment. If we get lucky, and we wrap this one up, then I'll let you know you can start breathing easy again. Until then if you're not panting like a randy St Bernard on a promise then I'll want to know why.'

Valentine eased himself onto the edge of the desk in front of him, indicated DS Donnelly to the front of the crowd. 'You're up first, Phil.'

'Thanks, boss,' said Donnelly. He stood, straight-backed before the gathered audience, then moved towards the board. He seemed to be waiting for his thoughts to align.

'Just the basics, Phil,' said Valentine. 'What have you got so far?'

'As you can see from the board, it's not a great deal, boss. There's been movement, some fact gathering but nothing very much in the way of progress.'

'Tell us about the prints analysis, what did the dusters come up with on the bloodstained wall?'

'The smeared lines on the wall, yes, that's been interesting.'

Valentine turned to face the room. 'On the night of the incident we were a little perplexed by these marks.' He retrieved the photographs from the board, passed them around. 'We couldn't make out if the marks were the work of one or two people.'

Donnelly spoke: 'If it was one, we surmised, one perp. But if it was two . . .'

'Two sources for the marks means two people fleeing the scene, two possible perpetrators. Of course there's no guarantees either way, could still have been one perp and a bystander, but that bystander may have been an accomplice or an active participant in murder.'

DS Donnelly watched as the photographs made their way around the room. 'Unfortunately, the dusters didn't come up with much. They're prints, for sure. But they're too smudged to be decipherable. There's a slight chance that some of the boffins in Glasgow might be able to enhance the limited info we have, blow the prints up so to speak, and look for matches but that relies on our perp, or perps, being on record. Sorry, boss, not what you wanted to hear, I'm sure.'

'How far down the queue are we with Glasgow?'

'They know it's a murder job, they've assured us of priority.'

'Well, thankfully there's precious few Old Firm games at the moment, but I won't get my hopes up.'

'I'll keep pressing them, sir.'

Donnelly collected the photographs, returned them to the board. 'The other aspect I was looking at was the murder weapon.'

'How did that go?' said Valentine.

'Well . . .'

'Oh, Christ. Go on.'

'Nothing retrieved by uniform. They carried out a full eyeball of the grassy patch at the end of the street – and the path to and from – but nothing. It's a well-trodden path, sir, main ingress and egress to the town centre for the scheme. I'd be surprised if anything showed up because it's very flattened land, and grass of more than a few inches in height is non-existent.'

Valentine looked at the DS. 'The place was heaving with people on the night, kids running about all over the shop, if that's even a fraction of the foot-traffic then I'd be surprised if a weapon lasted more than five minutes on that path.'

'It's Whitletts as well, if it's not tied down it wanders,' said DS McAlister.

Valentine agreed. 'All right, we're not giving up just yet, before someone mentions magpies liking a nice shiny blade as well.'

'Uniform went all the way into the town, sir. Along the banks of the river, they were pretty thorough. We had the bins too, before the scaffies emptied them out.'

'And has anyone searched the River Ayr?' said the DI.

No one answered.

Donnelly exhaled loudly, pursed his lips like he was about to whistle.

'Is that some kind of reaction to the costs, Phil?'

'We'd need divers for that, boss. A search of the river, I mean.'

'Well I wasn't expecting to do it with my old Woolies snorkel. Get on it, get the frogmen down there right away. If it glints, or has a pointy bit on the end, grab it.'

'Yes, boss.'

'And, Phil. Don't mention this to Dino, she's on a need-to-know basis. By that I mean needs to know bugger all unless it's been run by me first.'

DS Donnelly was writing on his clipboard, didn't look up.

'OK, Ally, what's your story?' said Valentine.

14

As DS McAlister walked towards the incident board Valentine removed the cap from a red marker pen. There was a list of the chores he had handed out at the murder scene with the relevant officer's initials beside them on the stark whiteboard. Under DS Donnelly's tasks he drew a fat zero and underlined it, twice.

'No disrespect to you, Phil,' said Valentine, 'you had the hard yards to cover for the rest of us.'

'Appreciated, sir,' said Donnelly.

'But we have to keep a tally so that we know where we are.' He paused as he returned the pen to the shelf below the board. 'We're a team, remember that, we work together not against each other, and *our* results are just that . . . our results. The only way we're going to crack this is by pulling together, sharing information and sticking it on the board as and when we have it.'

'Yes, boss.'

Valentine turned to McAlister. 'Right, Ally, you're up.'

The DS was still looking at the fat zero in red. 'I'm thinking there's not much by way of solid information that I can add, but there is some.'

'Many a mickle maks a muckle, as my old mam used to say.'

'Yes, boss.' He opened out the blue folder in front of him and started to engage the team. 'Well, as you'd expect, from the door-to-door, uniform picked up a lot of stuff, some of it's not much better than gossip, but some of it might turn out to be useful.'

From the folder McAlister removed a postcard-sized photograph of a girl in school uniform and held it up. 'Jade Millar – from the tie you'll gather she's a Belmont Academy pupil.'

He put the picture on the board.

'What year is she in, Ally?' said DS McCormack.

'Third year I think. Waiting on the department of education records coming over. But she's fifteen years old, so third or fourth year seems about right.'

'Why Belmont? Seems a bit of a schlep from Whitletts?' said Valentine.

'Yeah, well, the school was knocked down and rebuilt a few years ago and has some kind of mega-academy status now. They draw from all over Ayrshire.'

'Sounds like a recipe for disaster if you ask me, wouldn't want my kids mixing it with with the Ant Hill Mob . . . Have you spoke to her teachers, yet?'

'No, sir. I thought you'd like to come along for that.'

'Being a man of learning you mean?'

'Erm, I was thinking more of you being a man with teenage daughters – you could translate for us.'

A murmur of laughter spread throughout the room.

'Better revise your Taylor Swift lyrics, sir,' said McCormack.

'Christ we're in trouble if it comes to that. Right, Ally,

stick Jade up beside her brother and tell us what else you got.'

'Yes, boss.' McAlister flitted between board and folder for a moment and then continued his speech. 'Right, what we have on Jade is pretty minimal, not much to report on the door-to-door. But there's a lot more about her brother, Darry.'

'How so?'

'Well, Darry's been around longer, have him at about twenty-four, twenty-five and he's a kent face. Jade, much less so. Keeps herself to herself, quiet sort of kid, or so they say.'

'Boyfriend?'

'Yes, there's a young lad. We have a description but no name. We have a best friend for her too, girl called Alena from school. Should have home address by now, they sound pretty inseparable.'

'Set up a visit to Alena at home.'

'Yeah, will do. Oh, and we have a sighting of Jade on the night, about an hour or so before everything kicked off.'

'At the home?'

'No, the locus, though. Neighbour spotted her across the road on her mobile. That was about a half hour before the screaming started, but she's not been seen since.'

Valentine reached over for the red marker, grabbed it. 'Catch!'

'What do you want me to write up, sir?'

'Missing teenager.' He watched the pen's tip mark the board. 'And let's get on this missing teen now. Preferably

I'd like her found before the press cotton on and we have that to worry about too.'

'Yes, boss. The mother's still missing as well. That's Sandra Millar. She's forty-five and a widow.'

'What happened to the father?' said Valentine.

'Natural causes by all accounts, heart attack or stroke, seems to be some disagreement on the exact cause of death amongst neighbours. He passed a few years ago now, eight years to be accurate. He was a mechanic out at Baird's, long serving so they say and a salt-of-the-earth sort of bloke. Everything seemed to go a bit awry for them after he went.'

DI Valentine twisted round to talk to the team. 'A deceased father and a mother with a teenage girl to raise. Living in Whitletts and not exactly living well, she hooks up with a new bloke and he ends up murdered in her kitchen. What's the story?'

'According to uniform the pair of them had form for rowing,' said Donnelly. 'Not nightly, but not far off it.'

'But Darry had form for that too, I saw that on Agnes Gilchrist's statement,' said DS McCormack. 'There was something said about it getting a lot quieter since he joined the army.'

'So was he running amok for his mother, with no father in the home? Or, was it something more specific? Conflict with his mam's boyfriends, perhaps? We need to find this out.'

Pencils scratched on paper pads as the DI returned his gaze to the front.

'Thanks, boss.' McAlister stared at the photograph of the victim. 'Now, by all accounts, James Tulloch is a bit of a dark horse. Very few with much to say about him. There'd been words exchanged with the neighbours and none of them were on nodding terms. We believe he worked nights, somewhere in the town centre – I'm guessing maybe a bar or club – but that's not been confirmed yet. His record is patchy enough, a lot of motoring convictions and an aggravated assault that led to a court order to avoid the family home.'

'Not this home?' said Valentine.

'No. Previous address and a previous partner.' He flipped through the file. 'There's more here if you want it, erm, drunken disorderly, actual bodily harm. Seems a bit of a brawler on the quiet.'

'Pull his army record. They'll mess you about, but ask nice and you never know. Right, if that's your lot, Sylvia can run through what we picked up at the post-mortem.'

DS McCormack was shifting her way to the front of the crowd, holding up a page in her spiral-bound notebook as she went. When she reached the board, took over from McAlister, she pressed the page next to the photograph of Darren Millar. 'Sir, before I detail Tulloch's injuries, can I show you this?'

'And what's that?' said Valentine. 'Looks like you've been doodling.'

'That's my drawing of the tattoo on Tulloch's arm, the one Wrighty identified for us.'

The significance of the find reached the DI's face, he rose from the edge of the desk and grabbed the notepad, started to compare the drawing to a badge on Darren Millar's beret. 'What was it Wrighty called them?'

'The Royal Highland Fusiliers.'

'That's them.' He turned from the page to the board. 'Bit of a coincidence Darry the lad and his mam's boyfriend being in the same regiment.'

'Especially with one being dead and the other being missing,' said McCormack.

15

Grant Finnie gulped at the fresh, cold Arran air. They said it went through you, it didn't matter how many layers of clothes you wore. He put his bag down on the pavement outside the ferry port, then snatched it up again, held tight to the handle. There was a taxi coming and the driver seemed to have spotted him, was slowing down.

'Where can I take you?' said the driver.

'One of those B&Bs down the front.'

'No shortage of those in Brodick, OK . . . Want to chuck that bag in the boot?'

Finnie looked to the rear of the car, shook his head. 'No, it's fine with me here.'

As he opened the passenger's door, stepped inside and positioned the bulky holdall on his knees, the driver watched, patiently. 'Ready to go?'

Finnie nodded.

'A B&B it is.'

The drive was quiet, once Finnie had let it be known he wasn't feeling talkative. He didn't need the tourist spiel about trips to Goatfell and Brodick Castle, he knew the place well enough already. The cabbie was only after a tip, you could tell. The eager ones got chatty, in case you were the chatty type, but if they sussed you preferred quiet then they soon shut up. They'd concentrate on making you comfortable, heater up or window down, that kind of chat he could handle.

'Here we go, she keeps a tidy house in there.' The taxi driver pointed to a substantial sandstone villa with a short pebbled drive, three floors of net curtains and a large *Vacancies* sign hanging in the front window.

'That'll do,' said Finnie. He handed over the cash and waited for his change.

On his way towards the front door Finnie tried not to think about the circumstances which had brought him here. He didn't want to examine the events of recent days closely. He wanted to forget them completely, but that wasn't possible.

He pressed the doorbell and waited. It was strange being back in Brodick. The place seemed familiar, the crazy golf on the main drag, the cycling lycra-wearers clogging the roads. Had he ever been away? The answer was yes, the time in between was not something that could be rubbed out, certainly not now. It did seem strange though, coming back to his past when so much of his thought had been stuck there lately.

'Hello, sir.' The woman was a pale blonde in her fifties, she had the stout frame some settle for in middle age but it didn't suit her bearing. As she ushered Finnie inside, made a fuss of registering and form filling, the petty bureaucracy showed her priggishness.

'Is that us done?' said Finnie.

'Yes. That's the formalities aside,' she handed over a key, 'I do hope you'll enjoy your stay on the island.'

'Thank you.' The words sounded automatic, carried no connotation. He hoped she would rate him as just another gruff Glaswegian, or some other Central Belt scruff. He didn't want to draw attention to himself, so for once the stereotype was welcome.

At the foot of the stairs something beyond the front door caught Finnie's attention, in the window a white car marked *police* was crawling along the road. For a few seconds he followed its slow path and when it fell from view he went back to the stairs. His returning glance caught the landlady's, she continued to watch him as he went to his room.

Inside, Finnie flattened his back against the door and started to slump towards the floor. His head was heavy, lolling on his shoulders before his chest took the weight from his neck. He raised the holdall onto his thighs and tucked up his legs, clutching both bag and legs with his tight-gripping arms. It was not a comfortable pose but he held it for several minutes before the cold started to insinuate itself beneath the door, forcing him to rise.

'What the hell am I doing here?' he said.

He moved into the room, still clutching the holdall. As he reached the bed, with the white sheets tucked tight at the corners above a rosy valance, he lowered the bag and looked at his hand. The palm was red, deep-lined and moist with sweat. He opened and closed his fingers a few times then dug nails into the itchy palm.

The place was too open, too visible. He went to the window and closed the curtains. Enough daylight escaped the street outside to fill the room but he flicked on the electric light to chase away shadows. The large bed dominated the room, and the bag dominated the bed. He couldn't bear its presence, lunged for it, shoving the holdall below the bed, kicking the handles as they poked beneath the florid valance.

Finnie was still kicking as a noise began inside his coat pocket. He extracted the mobile phone with two fingers and held it before his eyes. The caller ID showed it was Norrie Leask. He dropped the phone on the bed and waited for the ringing to stop. When the ringtone ended the silence felt unnatural, then two sharp tones sounded to indicate a message had been left on voicemail.

He collected the phone from the bedspread and opened the inbox.

You have 62 unread messages waiting.

Scrolling through the list showed most were from Norrie Leask but there was also a number from Darren Millar, and one at the top of the list from Darry's sister, Jade.

The sight of the young girl's name in his phone set Finnie's hand trembling. His thumb hovered over the contact number for a few seconds but as his throat constricted and tears fell from his eyes, he could not dial the number.

'Where the bloody hell are you, Jade?' He hardly recognised the weak voice, shrill with emotion, it sounded like a child's.

The image of himself that his mind conjured forced a check on his actions. He smeared the tears from his cheeks, tweaked the end of his nose, and returned to the phone. This time, he went into his messages and listened to the last one from Leask.

'Now come on, Fin, you have to answer these calls

sometime. You know who this is, again. I'm not going to pretend I'm a happy man with you, Fin, you've let me down badly. You've let yourself down, Fin. Now it's not too late to turn around, wherever you are, and bring back what's not yours. I'm not going to try and fool you that there won't be consequences, but nothing you can't handle, just some face-saving for me . . .'

Finnie lowered the phone, screamed, 'You don't scare me, you bastard.' His heart accelerated as he gripped the phone and returned to the message.

'. . . Don't make me come looking for you, that's an expense I don't want, and one that I will take out of your hide, boy. I won't lose face for you, Fin. Not on your life. You can be guaranteed of that. Now, I do know I put a lot of temptation in your way and I can see I made a mistake there, you're obviously not the man I thought you were. But if you let me have it back, we can still stay the course with the plan. What we all agreed. You know that's best for everyone, well nearly everyone, of course. You know it's too late for . . .'

Finnie threw the phone at the bed, it burrowed into the pillows.

His voice came high and firm. 'Bastard. Who do you think you are, Leask? Playing the hard man with me, you don't know hard. You don't know me. You don't know what I've seen and done. You're nothing. Nothing. A tin-pot gangster. A bloody fantasist. I've met the real thing. I've done evil, Leask . . . You're nothing. You don't scare me.'

As he paused, Finnie became aware of knocking on the other side of the door. Slow at first, but gaining in persistence.

16

Chloe faced her father through the open car window and tugged her school bag tight to her shoulder. 'Why are you here and not Mum?'

'Why not?'

'Just asking.'

'That's not much of an answer, dear.'

'Well, it's just wrong.'

She looked back to the school building, pupils were rushing about in every direction, yelling, screaming.

'Come on, get in. It's like Bedlam out there.' He started the engine. 'I'm heading that way anyway, your mum was busy.'

The bag got jerked from her shoulder, she looked skyward and stomped for the passenger door of the car. Inside, the door slammed shut, Chloe threw her school bag onto the back seat. For a moment, she stared there, as if the bag had burst or flown out the window, and then she turned. 'You'd think they'd have given you another car.'

Valentine spluttered a line of laughter. 'Why would they do that?'

'Because of the . . . mess.'

'The bloodstain you mean, you can say the word y'know, it's not going to install a depression in me.'

'It's just so wrong, I mean, you know that.'

'Chloe, at the best of times a car is an expensive piece of kit, with all the cutbacks in the country right now do you really expect them to scrap it because there's a stain on the back seat?'

Chloe reached for her seatbelt, tugged at the inertia reel. 'It's wrong. You nearly died, I mean did die. At work on the job, and they still expect you to drive the car where you lost all that blood . . . *all* your blood!'

The DI always tried to listen to his children. Ever since they were very small, their first mumblings and ramblings, it all seemed important to him. He didn't ever want to be the type of parent who dismissed their thoughts as just those of children. It was a duty, something a decent parent did. If he let that slip, what was left? Children learned fast and needed to know they were listened to, that they were important, otherwise they simply accepted the opposite. And that would have been his fault. There were too many damaged souls in the world, he'd met many of them, and the thought that he'd increase their tally – however inadvertently – with one of his own children was a deep hurt he couldn't entertain.

'What do you think my boss would say if I took your complaint to her?'

'That depends.'

'Depends on what?'

'Depends if she's a decent human being or not. If she valued you, and your family, she'd get you a new car.'

'It's a company car, I don't think family is that high on her list of considerations.'

'But it should be.'

'Does it bother you that much, Chloe?' He watched his daughter play with the hem of her skirt. Just what was the conversation really about? 'I'm sorry I missed your big night, love.'

'It's OK.'

'No. It's not OK at all. Not for me it's not. I wanted to be there, to see my little girl make her big stage debut.'

Chloe pressed herself further into the seat. 'It's the job again, isn't it? It's always the job.'

'Now you sound like your mother.'

'Oh, please.'

'Shall we get going? Can't miss your drama class if you're to be a movie star.'

On the road to Troon, Valentine let his daughter select a radio station that met with her approval. An insipid boyband's tune filled the car, a manufactured kind of music that made the DI ask what had gone wrong with the world? He kept his opinion to himself, though. There were times when he could get away with teasing his daughter about her musical tastes but this wasn't one of them. He wasn't under any pressure from her for missing the opening night at the theatre, she wasn't the type to make a point for the sake of it, all the pressure came from him. The core feeling inside that said he'd let her down, let Clare down and now he needed to make amends. It could be shoved away, forgotten about for now, but where it would go and what it would do when it got there was a worry to him.

'I don't know what Mum's got to be so busy with, it's not like there's a sale at TK Maxx or anything.'

'Come on, Chloe.'

'I mean it, she doesn't work. All she has to do is shop and run about with her friends now and again . . . Oh, and drive me and Fi to the odd thing.'

'She has your Granda to look after too, now.'

'Granda looks after himself, he'd clobber you for saying something like that.'

'Am I picking up a bit of a vibe here, Chloe?'

'Is that you trying to sound street?'

Valentine stared at his daughter. 'I am street.'

They laughed together. The enormous pressure eased away.

'Yeah, I'm pathetic, I know. But all dads are a wee bit.'

'Is it funny for you having Granda around again?'

'No. Not really. We never see each other, sometimes in the passing, like ships in the night.'

'That's what Mum says, you're like ships in the night.'

'Oh, right.'

'Is Mum OK, Dad?'

'What do you mean by that?' His answer was a delaying tactic, he knew Chloe was growing up fast, forming her own impressions now. Clare was hard work sometimes but he didn't want his daughter to know that, or if she was coming to the conclusion, he didn't want her to think it. Not just yet, anyway. Not whilst she was still a child and prone to rash judgements.

'Just, y'know. She gets worked up and that, like this theatre thing. It doesn't bother me really but Mum got upset.'

'Your mother's a sensitive one, Chloe. She cares deeply

about things, about you and Fiona and the whole family. She wants things to be right, all the time.'

'But it can't be can it? I mean, that's just magazines and that.'

'It doesn't stop her trying.'

'But it's pointless. Futile.'

'To you maybe, love, but to her it's the stuff of life. Everyone needs something to cling to, to make it all make sense. It doesn't matter what it is, for you it might become acting, and that's great but it doesn't have to be any greater than anybody else's stuff. We're all different.'

'But what about when she goes on about your job and makes you both upset, that's not right either. And that's her thing too, y'know.'

Valentine didn't like the way the conversation was going, the plan had been to spend a little time with his daughter and appease his wife but all he'd done was confirm for himself that every family's unhappiness was unique. That always trying to be the better parent was impossible when kids drew their own conclusions regardless. 'This is getting very deep for the road to drama class, is it not?'

Chloe put her heels on the rim of the seat, pulled her knees up to her chin. 'I can't talk to Mum about things like this. There's only you and Granda.'

'Now your Granda could talk the leg off an iron pot, on any subject.'

She seemed to sense his need to change the topic now. 'It's all right, Dad. That's all I wanted to say.'

'It is?'

'Yeah. It is.'

At the turn-off for Troon, on the road skirting the golf course, the boyband was replaced by Eminem and Valentine felt his faith in the future returning. At the drama class Chloe waved, dodged some puddles in the car park, and went inside the old red sandstone building. What went on inside, what constituted an acting lesson? He found he had no reference for it at all. It was impossible to answer, another of life's mysteries and one that he had no pressing urge to solve. As the Vectra rolled back to the road he tried to clear some headspace for the real purpose of his visit to Troon. It wasn't something he was looking forward to, or even cared for, but it did seem necessary. And, he wanted to appease DS McCormack.

The DI pressed the call button, spoke into the mic. 'Hello Sylvia, that's me just getting into town.'

'Hi, sir. I'm there already.'

'Good. I'll see you in five, then,' his voice fluctuated in tone, settled on low notes.

'Is everything OK, sir?'

A pause. 'Why wouldn't it be?'

'It's quite a big step. Are you really sure you're ready to go through with this?'

'Sylvia, don't expect me to bluff you with *I was born ready*, or *I'm ready for anything*. But I am ready, yes. I'm ready to get to the bottom of why the dead keep walking into my life.'

17

DI Bob Valentine locked the car and headed towards the pub. DS McCormack stood outside, beneath the alcove at the front door. She was wearing a short red windcheater and stonewashed jeans with trainers, she didn't look like police for once.

'Are you sure this is how you want to spend your time off?' said Valentine.

'It's only a half day, I'll hardly miss it.'

'Is he here?'

'I've no idea, I'm not the clairvoyant.'

The detective suppressed a tut. 'Is that supposed to be funny?'

'A bit.'

'Well, I'm laughing inside . . . a bit.'

The pair walked through the front doors and into the bar area. It was a traditional Ayrshire drinking den, a long bar that covered one wall of the room, rust-coloured quarry tiles lined the front of the bar before the floor gave way to hardy, black carpeting that was beer-soaked and trampled to a sheen. Formica-topped tables, surrounded by PVC-backed chairs, accounted for the furnishings.

'Nice place,' said McCormack.

'I think it's what you call utilitarian.'

'Does that mean a tip?'

They approached the barman, his Brylcreem slick and black moustache fitted the fifties-feel of the decor. 'What can I get you?'

'Just a Coke for me,' said Valentine. 'Sylvia?'

'A mineral water, please.'

'No bottled water. I can do you a council juice from the tap.'

'Coke will be fine, thanks.'

They took their drinks and settled at a table near the back wall. The atmosphere was heavy and oppressive to the DI – he'd strayed into inhospitable territory. Valentine played with a Tennent's beer mat, picking the strayed edges.

'Are you nervous, sir?'

'Tell me about this bloke again.'

'Before the Janie Cooper case, like I said, I worked with a precognitive on the Reece squad in Glasgow. Colvin Baxter helped out, he took us in directions we never would have found on our own. It was a revelation. Baxter recommended Hugh Crosbie as someone who could, well maybe, help you get a handle on things, explain what you've been going through.'

'And this Crosbie, he's what, a psychic?'

McCormack sipped her drink. 'He's a spiritualist, as far as I know. He's very knowledgeable apparently.'

Valentine looked at his watch. 'He's also late.'

'I think we're a bit early actually.' The door to the bar opened, a tall man, thin and grey, approached. 'Oh, hang on, this looks like him.'

McCormack rose. 'Hugh, hello.'

He took the detective's hand, then turned to Valentine. 'And you must be Bob. I'm pleased to meet you.'

'Likewise.' He indicated the chair in front. 'Please, sit down.'

Valentine's gaze was drawn away from the man. He looked to the bar, spotted the barman resting on a stool and reading the *Daily Star*. It was a ridiculous scene, really. So prosaic and yet filled with such strange undercurrents. The urge to get up and leave instantly jumped into his thoughts.

'I'm forgetting my manners, would you like a drink, Hugh?'

'I'm fine, thank you.' He started to unbutton his jacket with long, slender fingers. 'I believe you've had some interesting experiences that you'd like me to give an opinion on.'

Valentine shifted uneasily in his seat. 'It's a little embarrassing really.'

'Oh. And why would that be?'

He didn't want to offend the man, he'd been good enough to answer the call after all. Even though it was all so strange to him, Valentine tried to affect manners. 'Perhaps that's the wrong word, unsettling maybe's a better one.'

'Go on.'

'I had this, I don't know what you'd call it, a near-death experience.'

'Did you die?'

Valentine picked up his glass, put it down again. He was used to the question by now. 'For a little while, I believe. I mean, I didn't see angels or anything if that's what you want me to say.'

'I don't think I've ever met anyone who has, met angels that is.'

'I was stabbed, in the heart. I passed away but they revived me. I don't recall anything of that time.'

DS McCormack entered the conversation. 'It's since the incident Bob's had the trouble. I say trouble because it's been troubling to him, unsettling.'

'You said something about dreams on the phone, and visions.' Crosbie got up to remove his coat, hang it over the back of the chair. When he sat down again he retrieved a notepad and pencil from the inside pocket and peered beyond the detective's shoulder.

'Mostly dreams. They're extremely vivid, like I'm actually there.'

Crosbie started to sketch in the notepad. 'Oh yes, spirit dreams can be most vivid. I believe some never forget them in their lifetime.'

'Well, I remember all of mine.'

'Are they precognitive dreams, Bob?'

'Do you mean, predicting the future? No, they don't give me the winner at the Gold Cup unfortunately.'

Crosbie smiled, a courtesy. 'Sometimes dreams like yours will contain a message and sometimes that message can be interpreted in a way that seems to have a forewarning attached. For example, I met a woman once who was convinced she had seen her daughter pass to spirit, actually holding hands with deceased relatives, the dream was so real she woke up in tears, ran through to the child's bedroom and woke her.'

'Did the girl die?' said McCormack.

'No,' said Crosbie. 'But what I found interesting about that dream, and many others, was that when the dead appear in such a state it's because they have something to tell you.'

'I'm not sure there was a message for me there.'

'I'm not sure you're interpreting it correctly, Bob.'

Valentine looked at the notepad as Crosbie glanced above him and sketched. 'And how would I do that?'

'You need to listen, not with your ears but with your soul. There's deep understanding there, not the kind you seek with your mind, but a fuller more complete wisdom. It's not a wisdom that can be explained in words, Bob, they would only get in the way. I think that's been your problem.'

'I'm not sure I understand.'

'Oh, I'm positive you don't. You see, it's not something you can understand with this,' he tapped the side of his head. 'You're trying to rationalise something that can't be subjected to the rational. That's your problem right there.'

Valentine looked at DS McCormack and then returned his gaze to Crosbie, he was tearing out a page from the notepad.

'Do you recognise this chap?'

He held up a sketch of a young man with short cropped hair and a prominent jawline. The picture was crude but a realistic impression.

'I'm sorry, I don't. Who is he?'

'I've no idea, Bob. But he's been standing at your shoulder since I came in.'

Valentine turned around. 'There's nobody there now.'

'Maybe he's not here for your benefit. Take the picture, it

99

might mean something to somebody, or it might mean nothing at all.'

'Thank you,' he took the sketch. 'I don't know what I expected, maybe that you'd be a nutter, or tell me that I was.'

'You're not a nutter, Bob Valentine. But you are a man who is a very long way from finding peace.'

18

Valentine pressed his fingertips into the hardwood desk and leaned forward. There was an expectant air inside the incident room, a haste and activity that forced everyone into quick steps and downward glances as they moved. The DI tried to ignore the goings-on and force his mind beyond the blurred morning state that could only cry out for coffee.

'It was the frogmen, I knew that was the risk we ran,' he said.

'Either way, boss, we'll have to give the hacks something,' said Donnelly. 'They're asking a lot of questions.'

'OK, there's no point keeping them in the dark when they know something's up. Ask Coreen to call a press conference, they can have the facts now, but only the bare minimum of stuff.'

Donnelly shuffled backwards towards the door. 'Yes, boss. When you say bare minimum, do you mean tell them we have a murder case but no more?'

'Definitely not. No names, no details beyond generalities. I doubt it'll take them more than a day to dig up the more salient facts but it's a day we can do with.'

Donnelly acknowledged the request and backed out of the office towards the press team. As Valentine lowered himself into his chair he signalled DS McCormack towards his desk with a crooked finger.

'Right. What have we got on this CCTV footage, Sylvia?'

McCormack stepped forward, tucking her hair behind her ear in a hurried, nervous manner. She started reading from a piece of well-thumbed notepaper as she walked towards the desk and the computer. She leaned over, pointed at the computer screen and said, 'Ally's put it on your desktop, it's the file called "River".'

He double-clicked on the file and a window opened up. It showed grainy footage of a slight figure – it looked like a woman – wearing jeans and a sweat-top, wandering awkwardly, almost feeling her way along the railings on the banks of the River Ayr.

'Do we have an ID?' said Valentine.

'No, we're working on enhancements. IT says we'll have those within the hour. If you want my best guess though – going on all our descriptions and the most recent photos – it's our missing Sandra Millar.'

'The mother.'

'Definitely fits the description, the height, colouring and clothes are all spot on . . . She's not exactly sprightly either, she moves like a middle-aged woman in shock.'

Valentine gripped his chin and scowled at the footage; it was good but he wanted more. 'It's a bit indistinct.'

'It's from the camera at Old Bridge Street, the operator was panning down the river banks, it's probably up to eleven on the focus.' McCormack touched the screen, tapped twice where she wanted him to look. 'Right this is where it gets interesting, sir.'

The figure in the centre of the screen stopped walking and turned towards the water. Her hands went out to the railing and she stood there, swaying for a moment. She seemed to be contemplating the river's movement, tuning in with the current, each ripple sending a shock that buckled her knees.

'Oh, don't tell me she's a jumper.'

'No. Keep watching.'

As the camera lens grappled with the image, going in and out of focus, the figure withdrew a hand from the rail. The task almost felled her but she straightened up, regained balance and managed to stand still. From the side of her that was blind to the camera she withdrew something from her pocket and raised up her arm. She paused, a glint appeared on the object, like a metallic surface catching a stray beam of light.

'What's she got?'

'It's what she does with it that's interesting.'

The figure jerked, her arm thrust back, and the object was thrown into the water. As a splash appeared in the river, the woman grabbed the rail again, then turned round and tramped towards the town. She followed the same route that she had come, her steps were heavy, faltering, and every uneven flagstone threatened her with a fall.

Valentine watched the woman's shambling gait go out of shot, then the image receded to a black screen. He closed the window and turned from the computer to face McCormack. 'Tell me you have the divers at that very spot.'

'Yes, sir. We have had them there for a while. But there's better news to report than that.'

'Go on.'

'About ten minutes ago, we retrieved an object from the River Ayr, adjacent to the banks where this CCTV image was captured.'

'Tell me it was a knife, Sylvia.'

She let a faint smile creep onto her face. 'Yes, sir. It's a blade. And it's making its way to forensics as we speak.'

Valentine shot up, raised a fist. 'Right, Sylvia. Get your coat. We're not hanging about waiting for the results on a potential murder weapon, especially when we have the press pack already baying for blood.'

The officers retrieved their coats from the stand in the corner of the DI's office and headed out into the open-plan incident room. DS Donnelly was approaching from the opposite end of the long room as they entered. He looked relaxed, pleased with himself. 'Boss, that's the press conference called. Coreen says she'll need you at midday.'

Valentine checked his watch. 'No can do. We're off to, hopefully, retrieve our murder weapon from the boffins in Glasgow.'

Donnelly looked perplexed. His confidence evaporated, 'But what about the press conference?'

'You can handle that, can't you?' Valentine's tone said he wasn't giving him a choice.

'Are you kidding? I've never faced the press on my own.'

'Then take Ally for company.'

The DI helped DS McCormack into her coat and through the door before Donnelly could object. Donnelly's gaze burned on the DI's neck as he walked into the corridor, but he didn't look back.

McCormack stayed quiet until they reached the station

car park: 'Don't think I'm questioning you, sir, but do you think it's a good idea leaving the Chuckle Brothers to face the press on their own?'

Valentine paused, pointed his keys at the Vectra. 'Needs must, Sylvia. And Donnelly will have to take that leap of faith at some time, might as well be today. He's a good lad, he'll rise to the occasion, and I'm sure he'll look out for Ally.'

They got into the car. Sylvia was stuffing her bag into the footwell as she replied to the DI. 'I was only thinking, what with Dino on the warpath already, now might not be the time to be courting tragedy.'

Valentine pushed himself into the headrest. 'Leave Dino to me, her bark's worse than her bite.'

McCormack's eyes widened. 'I just noticed on the case files that she's not been updated on the post-mortem findings either.'

'Our *coup de grâce*, you mean?'

'That's exactly what I mean.'

'Well, let's just say she's on a need to know basis. I'll let her know what I do when she needs to, until then there's no point overloading her, it just gets her twitchy about the cost of running a case like this.'

'Did you tell her we called in frogmen?'

Valentine started the car, over-revved. 'Look, no. I didn't. She'll find out today though, I'm sure of it.'

McCormack was shaking her head. 'I hope she doesn't find out at the press conference. She'll be standing in wait for you at the front door if she does, most likely with your P45 in one hand and a baseball bat in the other.'

19

Sandra Millar whispered her daughter's name to herself and listened as the wind snatched it away. On cold mornings like this, when Jade appeared barefoot and shivering in her kitchen, she'd hug her tight, tell her to wrap up before going out. She never listened though. Never ceased to pad about the house barefoot or wear a decent coat to go down the street. It was her age, teenagers were like that, but there was more to it as well.

It seemed like such a long time since Sandra had been with Jade, old memories were welling up, but it might have been only a few hours. Everything was unreal now, thoughts appeared clear and bright and immediately became foggy. Jade in her little red boots, the boisterous two-year-old wanted to wear the boots to bed, screamed at all attempts to remove them, and then she was gone. A sulky teenager showed up, dourly locked herself in her bedroom to listen to The Pistols. The good times and the bad. Why hadn't there been more of the good? Why hadn't she done more to make her daughter happy, keep her safe? Sandra shoved away her thoughts, shut her eyes. When she opened them again reality had returned.

The scene was familiar enough, she knew the streets, recognised the buildings, the faces hadn't changed. But nothing was as it appeared. As new thoughts started bubbling up, banging in her head, Sandra stumbled along the street to escape them. But they followed her; it was as if she was being chased out of her own mind.

'Watch yourself there, dear.' An old man, he held out a hand like he was offering help. 'Everything OK, love?'

Sandra looked away, continued up the High Street. People were staring, she was making a show of herself – that's what the looks said. Her head throbbed, it was hard to think. All she could see were strange pictures floating in and out of her mind. Jade mostly but there was James Tulloch too. He was dead now. The knife in him, the blood, he must be dead. There were screams and wails. She could hear them still, something terrible had happened. Something so awful she couldn't see it now, it was as if she'd blocked the incident out. It had to be locked away, hidden, because to ever face it meant accepting the most overwhelming pain.

'No, no, no,' said Sandra. She knuckled her temples and carried on up the street, a channel forming through the crowd as people stepped out of her way.

'Jade!' she called out, not quite a shout but above her normal range.

People turned, some stopped and stared. A group of young boys jeered, they were just kids, in tracksuits with football scarves tied to their wrists. 'Missus, who let you out the loony bin?'

Sandra cried, immense coldness welling inside her, and started to run. Her steps were long, loping, but soon she was slipping on the wet street. She didn't know where she was running to. There were too many lights. Too many people. The rain, the wet, and the crowds. The jeering kids, they were everywhere. No matter how fast or far she ran there was no escaping the horror. People stared, they spoke in strange voices. Sandra felt threatened, like she was being hunted. She stopped running, her legs too heavy, her ankles and feet numb.

Falling was sudden but once begun never seemed to stop. The drop was too slow, she wanted the blow of the pavement to come though there were too many images in the way. Jade and James Tulloch flashed again, the blood, and the knife.

The slap of her head on the concrete came with a scream, but it was hers this time, not some long forgotten hurt of her daughter's that had hung around her memory. Sandra lay still, let the raindrops tap her face, then curled into a ball outside the entrance to Smith's.

A man stepped over her motionless body, another walked around her.

'Jade. Why?' she whispered to the wet ground.

A woman crouched. A low voice, calm but distinct. 'Is everything OK?'

She didn't reply. They were just words, she couldn't process their meaning.

More sounds came. A jumble of voices.

'I think she's had a stumble.'

'She's given herself a knock on the head.'

'I saw her running up the street, she was all over the place.'

'I think the poor soul's lost . . . Love, are you OK there?'

Sandra pulled up her knees. She wanted to be away. She wanted to be somewhere where she was invisible, where she could hide from the world and where nobody knew what was going on inside her. Where nobody else could find out what she had seen. But the images kept coming, and people continued to gather around her.

'Has someone called an ambulance?'

'Or the police? Someone should make a call.'

Sandra called out. 'Jade . . . Jade . . .'

'What's she saying?'

'I don't know, sounds like someone's name.'

Sandra shrieked as a cold hand was pressed on her wet brow. 'We've called the ambulance, dear. They'll be here soon.'

Who were they? Why were they fussing around? Sandra eased herself up, crouched against the wall. She pulled up her legs, her knees were scuffed and reddened. There was blood, patches of it, dark black scars and long red lines running down to her shins. On her hands too, she stared at them. They were red with blood and black crescents under the nails. She held them in front of her eyes, her long white fingers trembling, and cried out again.

'Jade. My daughter . . .'

'What's that?'

'I want my daughter. She needs me.'

A woman in a white woollen hat leaned towards her, the glasses on her nose were wet with the rain and blurred her eyes. 'Don't worry yourself, the ambulance is coming. You've had a nasty fall, given yourself quite a knock.'

'No!' It wasn't the fall that Sandra cared about. There

were other pointers to how she came to be curled up in Ayr High Street, with a small crowd gathering around her, poking and prodding her as she cried for her daughter. Everything was fragmenting, the memories, the pictures of horrors she didn't understand. Blood and wounds. A blade. Screams. Her daughter's face, twisted in tears. Her boyfriend's bloodied back slouched at the table in her home. It was unreal but so familiar, like a scene from a movie she'd seen a hundred times but couldn't quite piece together the plot.

'James is *dead*,' she cried.

'What?'

'James is dead.' Sandra sobbed into her dirty hands as the rain washed blood onto the street. The sight of the blood made her thrust her hands away but she couldn't escape the terror. She pushed herself from the ground, grabbed at the wall and scrabbled through the crowd. She was on the road, running awkwardly. New sounds started behind her.

A screech of brakes.

'Watch out!'

'Stop.'

A burn of rubber.

'It's hit her . . .'

20

There was a niggle bothering DI Bob Valentine. For the first time, or so it appeared, things were going their way on the case. If the knife turned out to be the murder weapon, and the forensics team could find fingerprints in the bloodstains on the wall, then he would have something to take to the chief super that might calm her down, maybe put him on her good side. CS Martin was a simple enough sort to play. Providing he prefaced all bad news with a greater quantity of good news, she tended to be sufferable. It was all pride with her. If the CS had something she could take upstairs, and earn a few plaudits for, then she could be quite easy to please.

'You're looking chuffed with yourself,' said McCormack.

Valentine glanced towards his passenger. 'Think we've left at just the right time, rush hour's cleared right up.'

'Was I being too optimistic thinking it might be the case that had started to cheer you up?'

'You'd have to be a funny old sort to be cheered by a murder investigation, Sylvia.'

'I meant the progress.'

He steered the Vectra through the curve of the road, evacuated a spray of pooling rain water. 'I'll be happy when we have the murderer in custody, until then my dancing shoes can stay where they are.'

Valentine didn't want to think about how far they had come on the case. Rewarding himself for every achievement led to a false sense of gain when there was no real victory to be had. A life had been taken and many other lives disrupted and affected by the actions of a killer. His town, where he lived and raised his children, would only be a safer place once that killer had been caught and removed from the streets. It was not a task to be treated lightly. It was the role he had given everything to, and had nearly cost him his life. There was no way of approaching a murder investigation softly and now that the press conference had been called a new set of pressures were about to begin.

Those in the less functional uniforms, with the shiny buttons and big caps, tended to get nervy when closely scrutinised by the media. Demands were put on investigating officers and workloads and stress levels increased. Things like leave got cancelled. Enforced overtime became the norm. The station, and others like it, became inhospitable places where dour officers passed each other in grim obsession. Everyone knew the light would only return to their lives when the case was closed. The panic reached the public eventually too, and if it was left alone, made for a dangerous atmosphere that spilled into areas it shouldn't. When that happened, the killer was in control, harboured delusions of omnipotence that increased the danger for everyone. Fear ruled then.

Nobody liked to think of a murderer walking their streets – you couldn't contain news like that for long, though. In the days to come, Valentine saw himself fending off prying questions from neighbours, posed over the garden wall, and if he didn't have the right answers, in a quick enough fashion, he'd become a part of the fear himself. He didn't want to think like this but it was his job, not just as an officer, but as a husband and father, a member of his community. His wife should have no more to worry about than their children and their biggest fear should be from exam results. No one deserved to live in fear of a killer.

The DI's mobile phone interrupted his thoughts.

'Want me to get that, sir?' said McCormack.

'No, just leave it to go through the speaker, it's on the Bluetooth.' He answered the call. 'Hello, Bob Valentine.'

'Hello, there.' He didn't recognise the voice, the accent was too rarefied for his circle. 'I'm Major Rutherford . . .'

The gap on the line was a ruse for Valentine to reveal his position, but he didn't bite. Experience, or guile, had taught him to play the chippy bloke's role in these situations; it got results.

'Yes,' said the DI. 'And how can I help you, Major?'

'I had an interesting telephone conversation with one of your subalterns recently, Inspector. I believe his name was McAlister; the chap said you were conducting a case where one of my boys had been mentioned, Darren Millar.'

'It's a murder investigation.'

'I see. And has Millar's name been linked to the crime in any sort of nefarious way? You understand the regiment would need to be kept informed of any implications.'

'Implications?'

'I mean for the regiment. He's one of our boys but we

have a duty to uphold the good name of the Fusiliers, you understand.'

The major's tone began to grate. What was it about a certain class of people that they excluded themselves from the norms of politesse that the rest of us obeyed? 'You'll understand a murder investigation is a very sensitive affair and I'm bound by strict regulations and procedures.'

'Of course, but we are both seeking the same end, as I said.'

'I don't see how, Major. I'm hunting the killer, not your missing squaddie. And if I was, I wouldn't be discussing that with anyone in any way unrelated to the case.'

The line fizzed.

'Inspector, I don't want to get off on the wrong hoof, so to speak. I'm sure we can both be of assistance to each other in this case.'

'Of course. And I'd like to speak to you about Darren Millar, how does tomorrow sound?'

'What about today? I'm in your area for the next little while, I could be with you inside an hour.'

'I'm sorry but I'm not in the office at the moment.'

'In that case, is there somebody else? McAlister perhaps?'

'He's conducting a press conference today, I'm afraid.'

'Not about the Darren Millar case, the press call, is it? I should think I'd really need to be present for that.'

Valentine glanced at McCormack, her mouth tightened. The embarrassing gall of the man might not have been close to Prince Phillip asking an Aboriginal elder if his people still chucked spears at each other, but it attracted the same derision. 'Look, as I've said, Major, this is a murder

114

investigation. Darren Millar is an integral part of our inquiry but this is not a joint inquiry we're holding with the Royal Highland Fusiliers.'

The major's voice rose, seemed to indicate an escalation of more than volume. 'Valentine, who is your superior officer?'

The DI spotted McCormack fanning her hand over her mouth. He kept the tone of his reply consistent but the limits of his endurance had been surpassed. 'I don't believe I have one, Major. If you want my next in command, that would be Chief Superintendent Marion Martin and you can reach her through the switchboard at King Street station.'

Valentine ended the call, switched off the phone speaker.

'What a total dick!' said McCormack.

'I bet he gets on great with Dino. Do me a favour, just unplug that mobile altogether, and the radio, would you?'

'Is that wise? You know she'll go bananas if she can't get hold of you.'

'Well, I'll know it's serious if I see blue lights flashing in the rear-view, Sylvia.'

21

DI Bob Valentine was uncomfortable in the Glasgow lab. It didn't matter how many times he visited the place, it always felt unfamiliar. The faces changed too regularly and the white, clinical feel seemed to repel any attempt to humanise the area. No one looked happy in their starched coats, shuffling around in silence like extensions of the furniture or the equipment. The lab was like a temporary affair, like the set of a movie or a greenhouse that was only useable in the summertime, no one wanted to lay claim to it or make their mark there. In the other areas of the station, the offices, even the morgue, there were hints of humanity: coffee cups, pot plants and pictures of children. There was none of that here.

'So cold, isn't it?' said Valentine.

'I guess so. Never really thought about it,' said DS McCormack.

'I get the feeling that if someone came in here with a pastie from Greggs the alarms would go off.'

'It's a clean room, it has to be spotless.'

'I couldn't work here.'

'Because you're not spotless.'

'Well, there's no flies on me, but I'm far from spotless, Sylvia.'

The officers were directed to a seating area – hard blue plastic chairs – Valentine chose to stand.

'Mike'll be with you in a minute, he's just printing off some of the data.' The unsmiling twenty-something in the long white coat backed out of the door.

'Where do they get them?' said Valentine. 'They seem like an altogether different species.'

'They're boffins, sir. It's all those years of study that could have been spent out honing social skills.'

'You mean while we were on the death knocks by day and the bevvy by night this lot were staring into test tubes and frothing beakers.'

'And you called it your misspent youth, when really, it was all your societal assimilation.'

Valentine digested the remark, alighted on a choice memory from Ayr's Bridge's Bar but kept it to himself. 'Makes sense. Schooling of sorts. I don't know that my days of yore would stand me in good stead for a job in here, though.'

'Horses for courses. We're all toiling for the same thing now.'

'Well, let's just hope their microscopes have picked up something we've missed.'

Valentine consented to remove a blue plastic chair from its resting spot and sat opposite the DS. The little room was a slightly less sterile extension of the lab with, almost a concession to decoration, a health and safety notice behind Perspex on the wall.

The officers were growing restless as the door's hinges wheezed and Mike Sullivan entered.

117

'Bob, Sylvia, good to see you both.'

Valentine leaned out of his seat but was motioned back down. 'No, stay where you are, you can have a look at this.' Sullivan placed a blue folder on the table.

'Don't tell me you've typed a report already, Mike.'

'Eh, no . . . that's my notes from the lab. You'll get the full report in due course, most likely after I've digested lunch and wee Kenny through there's got to the word processor.'

'Before we get to this, Mike, I was hoping to get the latest on what your team have made of the crime scene.'

'Oh, yes. The blood smears and prints, that should be with you later today too. I'll get Kenny to fire that over with the new notes.' Sullivan put his hands in his pockets and, just as quickly, removed them. 'Look, we've not found much that's going to be of use to you, Bob.'

'Go on anyway,' Valentine looked at McCormack, 'anything you say is an addition to what we have.'

'OK, then. I can confirm the blood in those smears is definitely all from the victim, the samples match.'

'Well I didn't expect the perp to leave any claret at the scene, there was no indication of a struggle, didn't even knock the sugar bowl over.'

'Apart from the smear lines on the wall it all looked very clinical,' said Sullivan.

'And any prints from the smear lines?'

'We only recovered one full set of prints. Female. And, Bob, I'm sorry but she's not on record.'

'Bloody lovely, that. And there was me getting my hopes up.'

'We got fairly good enlargements from the wall plaster, that should be of some use to you.'

'If we find their owner, you mean.' Valentine leaned forward to pick up the folder and scan the contents; his hopeful gaze raced. 'A serrated-edge knife.'

'Well that matches, there were scraping wounds,' said DS McCormack.

'I'd sooner it matched a set from the kitchen, the missing one from a complete set, and that it had fingerprints on it.'

Sullivan spoke: 'We've not been that lucky, Bob.'

'I see that,' he held up a page, 'no trace evidence recovered.'

'Nothing to link to the killer. Certainly not at this stage.'

Valentine shoved in the stray page and threw down the folder. 'Meaning?'

'I mean, it's possible we could recover blood or tissue beneath the handle but we haven't got that far yet, it's a lengthy process and there's still a few options before we get there.'

'I'd need a killer in custody to make that stick, preferably with a confession unless their DNA's on there too.'

Sullivan retrieved the folder from the table, patted down the pages and tucked it under his arm. His tone was breathy, carried on the back of a sigh. 'That would be a long shot, all the samples I've seen taken from knives in water have been the result of deep blows into soft tissue, hard and repeated impacts. If we find anything now it's likely to be the victim's residue, not the one you're looking for.'

Valentine looked forlorn. 'There's nothing here for me to go on then?'

'I thought you had CCTV. Can't it be enhanced to ID the person with the knife?'

'I doubt it. I've more chance of our perp having taken a nick off the blade. Look, what are these options you've still to try?'

'Nothing to get excited about, Bob, just enhancing already perceived markings. There's some partial printing on the handle but if we can extract it then we've still got to match it to the database.'

'Or the prints from the blood smears.' DI Valentine rose and thanked Sullivan, they exchanged heavy handshakes. In the car park he was deep into his stride when DS McCormack called him.

'Hang on, sir.'

'Sorry, Sylvia, there's no point hanging around. Let's get back to the press conference, we might catch the tail end of it if we're lucky.'

She stopped still. 'I don't think you should be so disheartened, we can still get something from the boffins, they've got more to do.'

'Not in my experience.' He opened the car door. 'They either front up with plenty to help us right away or paper over their failings with promises of more to come.'

McCormack faced him over the car roof. 'If we do have a hot-blooded and angry killer, then of course you're right. They'll likely be known to their victim, family or friend, and may not have a record with prints on file we can match. But what if it's not?'

'What are you getting at?'

'I mean, what if it's a cold-blooded and calculated murder and the killer has form?'

They got inside the car. 'Very well, Sylvia, but you've forgotten one thing. The lab boys still need to find something *else*. And I'm not confident they will. The blade's clean, it's been in water for long enough to be even cleaner than when it was chucked away, the odds are well and truly against us.'

22

The A77 back to Ayr was quieter than usual, the occasional white van making itself conspicuous by speeding past the officers in their unmarked vehicle. Valentine knew there were some on the force who would pull over the offending driver – for their own entertainment more than anything – but the thought never appealed to him. Traffic offences were dealt with by an altogether different species from him, hardly police at all, merely civil servants who handed out fines and collected a wage for their bother. It wasn't that he looked down on this branch of the force, a job was a job and they all had to be done, but his own undertakings couldn't be compared. How could you weigh the loss of life, in brutal fashion, against a heavy foot on the accelerator pedal.

The DI found his thoughts focusing on the disappointment of the Glasgow lab visit. He was being foolish, placing such high expectations on forensic evidence. His job wasn't like the super cops on the television who find a speck of dust and everything was pieced together by men in white coats. It took solid police work, hard yards. No one was going to come and solve the murder for him, it was entirely his responsibility.

Thinking of the murder, the violent incursion of a blade

into the soft flesh of a living being brought home his own suffering. Not just the pain he felt but his family's pain. His wife and daughters' tears, his aged father's fatigued and worn look he carried for months. The worry they all shared. The ultimate act of violence was murder but it didn't stop with the corpse, its shockwaves echoed much farther afield.

The schoolgirl and her mother were still missing. Where had they gone? Would there be more victims cropping up soon? The girl was only fifteen; who was looking out for her? Valentine worried less about the brother, or should that be worried about a completely different set of issues. Darry Millar was army, a survivor. He hadn't deserted his regiment without cause – it was a huge step to take and the consequences were great. Darry was a worry to the DI not because he feared for his safety but because he feared for the safety of others; the thought of more victims piling up increased with each tick of the clock.

'We've almost drawn another blank,' said Valentine.

'It's still at an early stage, sir.'

The officers avoided eye contact.

McCormack continued. 'What I mean is, the initial findings have been minimal and I know you'd normally look out for your best leads in the first day or two but it's not like we haven't made any progress.'

'It's going to be uphill from here, Sylvia, we both know that.'

'We've little or no forensic, that's true, but not every case is solved quickly.'

Rain started to splatter on the windscreen, a grey smear was spreading from the Fenwick Moors. The DI turned on the wipers, they had little effect; he moved them up a notch. It was a grim picture, inside and out.

'I worry about the Millar girl,' he said.

'Me too.'

'She's only fifteen, just a bairn really.'

'She's not that young, I remember what I was like at her age, lusting after Morten Harket.'

'Lusting after what?'

'Not what, *who*. He was in a band called A-ha.'

'A-ha!'

'Very funny. What I'm trying to say is, the image you have of girls Jade Millar's age is probably heavily influenced by your daughters, little girls don't stay little girls for very long.'

Valentine took in the remark, let the words work on his mind. He didn't want to relate his fears for his daughters to the case, he'd done that once before and suffered for it. 'Do you remember what we went through on the Janie Cooper case?'

'Jade's not going to be another Janie – it's a completely different set of factors. She'll turn up.'

'Are you basing that on anything or is it just your women's intuition?'

DS McCormack smacked the dash. 'Just a wee bit sexist sounding, sir.'

Valentine promptly agreed. 'I'm teasing you, Sylvia. As you know, I'm not the most intuitive of folk. If I was I would be catching onto some of these hints your psychic pal Crosbie seems to think are flooding my way.'

'Did the picture he gave you start ringing any bells?'

'No, nothing. I meant to have another look before I left the house this morning but it passed me by.'

'Where is the picture now?'

'On the fridge. I stuck it there when I was grabbing a late tea.'

'Clare will think you've started to get all arty on her.'

Valentine laughed. 'I doubt that very much. She knows me too well.'

The rest of the journey passed in silence, except for the volume of rain pelting along the bypass. The DI played out possible scenarios for Jade Millar's whereabouts, stacked up the odds of Darry's involvement in shielding her from sight. Nothing was sitting right with the current situation, it was as if someone had cried murder and the household fled.

On the way into King Street station Valentine began to speak again. 'We need to go back to brass tacks, Sylvia.'

'Meaning?'

'We have to draw up detailed profiles, call in known associates.'

'You make them sound like criminals.'

'Well one of them is.' He held open the door for the DS.

'Not necessarily, sir. We could be looking for someone outside the family unit, someone we've missed.'

'True. But they'll be attached in some way. I want a thorough profile on all the known players: Jade, Darry, Sandra and our victim, Tulloch, too. What do we know about him, apart from the fact that he was in the army?'

'Not much, yet. The team's focus has been on collating the available facts from the scene.'

'We need to spread out our approach now, before things get away from us. Somebody knows something about this family and why Tulloch ended up on a mortuary slab and it's time for us to start rattling a few cages.'

'OK. I mean, you're the boss.'

At the foot of the stairs Valentine heard his name called.

'Bob, you're back to face the music, I see!' It was Jim Prentice, still behind the front desk.

The DI turned around. 'What are you on about, Jimbo?'

He leaned onto the desk, steadied himself on folded forearms. 'Something up with your radio? And your phone as well?'

'Have you been trying to get me?'

'Oh, you could say that. Tried covering your arse for you as well but when Dino comes down here and stands over my shoulder whilst the dead signal comes back it gets a wee bit difficult.'

Valentine directed Sylvia to the stairs. 'I'll gather the team, sir.'

'Jim, can you spare me the histrionics, eh?'

'Well I presume you never heard about the press conference that was crashed by Captain Mainwaring. Or should that be Major Mainwairing? Major bloody knob anyway.'

'Rutherford showed up?'

'Aye. That's not the best of it, though.' Jim unfolded his arms and raised himself before leaning closer to the DI as he approached. 'Your missing woman, the one with the dead boyfriend, well she's only gone and turned up . . . Just about put up a three ring circus in the high street!'

23

When DI Bob Valentine entered the incident room it was as if the pause button had been pushed. Heads turned and frenetic pacing stopped, mid-stride. The lull in the room's volume was less pronounced, but for a moment the street seemed to come closer, bringing with it the sounds of traffic and hard-hitting rain. Valentine stood in the doorway with the handle gripped tight in his fist, he had enough temper to slam the door shut, watch the dust bounce from above the skirting and see a few faces shriek but those days were gone. Giving into the whims of mood, in his condition, could be injurious to the already weakened muscle pounding inside his chest.

He removed his coat, placed it on the coat stand and made for the whiteboard where some of the DCs had gathered. 'Back to work,' he yelled. 'Unless someone's found a genie with three wishes going begging, we still have a murder to solve by our own efforts.'

DS Ally McAlister was the first to approach Valentine. 'Think we need to have a bit of a chat, boss.'

'Well let's hope it goes better than every other one I've had this morning.'

'Take it Jim's been on the tom-toms?'

'Waylaid on the doorstep, slavering like a cartoon dog

with a string of sausages, so he was.' Valentine pointed to the glassed-off office at the other end of the room. 'Ally, Phil, Sylvia . . . in there when you're ready.'

In his office, Valentine was greeted by a fresh scattering of yellow Post-it notes. He grabbed one, stuck it on top of another, and repeated the process till he had formed a little monument to the morning's messages. The note on top caught his attention: his father had called and wanted a return call.

Valentine picked up the phone, dialled 0 for reception.

'Hello, Jean, the message from my dad, was it urgent?'

'Bob, *hi*, no I don't think so. He'd tried your mobile but it was off . . . said something about a picture on the fridge you had left behind.'

'What?'

'That was it. Said he didn't want to call but curiosity had got the better of him.'

'That or he'd already seen today's rerun of Antiques Roadshow . . . I'll give him a bell later. Thanks, Jean.'

The rest of the notes followed a similar pattern. Missed calls to mobile. CS Martin had stacked up half a dozen of those on her own, each one with a pointer to the time of call which indicated she'd been keen enough to get hold of him that she'd rung every fifteen minutes for more than an hour. He was glad the calls seemed to have stopped, whatever her problem was he would need to give Dino time to cool off now before he did talk to her. A day or two would be ideal but he doubted that much time was available.

The office door opened, in walked Donnelly and McAlister.

'Where's, Sylvia?' said Valentine.

The DSs looked at each other, Donnelly chimed first: 'Lost your shadow, boss?'

Donnelly averted his gaze to the floor. For a moment, McAlister was left grinning to no one but himself.

'Is that supposed to be funny, Phil?' said the DI.

'Er, no. Well, just a gag, y'know.' Phil was not known for his sense of humour, Ally was the joker.

'I'd say stick to the police work, son, but I'm not sure that's your forte either. Is there something you have to say to me?'

Donnelly coughed on his words. 'The press conference went a little worse than I was expecting, boss.'

Valentine saw that the DS was nervous, he let the remark about McCormack go. 'You were anticipating the worst when I left, Phil, are you telling me you exceeded your own expectations?'

'It was the first press conference I've ever headed up.'

'Sounds like you're trying to lessen the blow – just tell me what happened.'

'The army showed up.'

'I'm assuming you don't mean the SAS.' Valentine shook his head.

'No. Just Major Rutherford. But he was enough.'

'Jim on the desk told me there'd been some kind of kerfuffle.'

DS McAlister moved towards the seat by the printer. 'Putting it mildly. We might have fared better if he'd actually abseiled through the windows with a squad of paratroopers.'

It was just a press conference, one of a thousand that had

been held at the station, so Valentine struggled to take in what his officers were relaying. 'Oh, come on. There's only so much can go wrong at one of these things, and most of it comes from the hacks.'

Donnelly pulled out the other spare seat, sat. 'It might not have been so bad if the chief super hadn't got right behind him. She actually came along and told us he was to take the lead . . .'

Valentine erupted, 'What? Are you bloody kidding me? Since when was this an army investigation?'

DS McCormack joined the group. 'Sorry, I was on a call. What have I missed?'

Valentine's bulging eyes, rimmed with red vessels, sent a stronger message than words.

'Or maybe I shouldn't ask?' said McCormack.

Ally retraced the main points of the conversation, added in the fact that Major Rutherford had asked that the Fusiliers be kept out of the picture for the moment and CS Martin had agreed.

'So we're supposed to just keep Darren Millar's involve-ment hush-hush?' said McCormack. 'That won't be easy for long.'

'He's someone we're seeking to *assist with our enquiries*,' said Phil. He'd loosened off his tie and now he removed it. 'It's bloody humiliating, not to mention the fact that our hands are tied as far as the investigation goes.'

Valentine got up, pushed out his chair, moved from behind his desk. 'That'll be bloody right.' He pointed at Donnelly and McAlister. 'I want the pair of you out at Glencourse Barracks tonight. I want the full SP on Darren

Millar, if he wet his bed once, I want to know. I want his every move cross-referenced with James Tulloch's and what kind of relationship they had, if any, in this regiment. And if Major Rutherford or Dino doesn't like that then they can take it up with the Home Secretary. Go, now!'

DS McCormack spoke: 'And what about me, sir?'

'You're staying here for the minute.' He checked Donnelly and McAlister for a reaction, continued: 'You and I are heading out to the hospital again, Ayr this time, to see what sort of sense we can get out of Darry's mother.'

'Sandra Millar turned up?'

'You could say that. More like thrust herself under the front wheel of a Suzuki scrambler some teenage lunatic was taking for a spin down the High Street.'

'Is she all right?'

'No, Sylvia, she's unconscious. But when that changes, she's going to have quite a few bloody questions to answer.'

24

Valentine grabbed his pinstripe jacket from the back of his chair and headed out after the DSs. He had toyed with the idea of ripping off his tie and wearing it round his head, Rambo-style, but selected the saner option of straightening the knot and fastening his shirt button. There was nothing to be gained from confronting Dino and Rutherford with hot blood, that would only give away his true feelings about this morning's goings-on and he wanted to build his case slowly. The DI knew his own defenestration was likely, he'd been exasperating the chief super for too long now, switching off the radio and his mobile phone was a step too far. She was prickly, thin-skinned was a phrase her enemies were fond of, and in anger she would side with anyone to get her own way; it was an extension of the old *your enemy is my enemy* rule. Of course, knowing any of this made no difference to the situation, it was impossible to gain an advantage on a person like Martin whose sole reason for being was to gain advantage over others. Even the thought of going to war with her exhausted the detective.

In the hallway Valentine went over his thoughts. His pulse was returning to normal now and the bitter taste he carried in his mouth had disappeared. If he could only hold his lip in check, his desire to speak his mind, then he might survive the encounter. He took a shallow breath and knocked on CS Martin's door. Nothing. Normally, there would be a curt call of 'come' or the sound of hard heels clicking across a harder floor before the door was yanked open, but this time his knocks were greeted with silence.

He knocked again. Harder this time.

Laughter, the sound of convivial voices.

'Sounds like a bloody cocktail party in there,' said Valentine to the empty hall; he was very much on the outside.

Another knock. And a resolve to open the door himself if he was ignored again.

The sweet tones from beyond the door came closer for a moment, then spilled out.

'Oh, hello, Bob,' said CS Martin, her relaxed demeanour was so unfamiliar to him that Valentine suspected he had the wrong door.

He peered over her shoulder. 'If it's not a good time, I can try later.'

A firm hand clutched his forearm, grabbed him into the office. 'No, now's fine. After all, we've been chasing you all morning, and a wee bit of the afternoon too.' Her smile hid the harsher truth of those words.

'I'm sorry, did I mention my murder investigation?' As he walked in Valentine spotted a highly polished brogue dangling from the end of a trouser leg that his late mother would have said held a crease that could cut butter.

'You won't have met Tom, will you?' said Martin.

'I think we spoke earlier.'

'Oh, yes?'

'On the phone.'

The brogue flashed into fuller view, was met by another at the heel. 'That must have been before you went off the radar, Inspector.' He thrust out a hand, awaited a shake. 'Tom Rutherford.'

Valentine met the hand in front of him. 'Well, I wasn't entirely AWOL, Tom . . . unlike Darren Millar.'

The chief super motioned the men to sit down, returned to her side of the desk and laced fingers, topped with pointed red nails, over the blotter.

As Valentine sat he tried to gauge the room's mood but the temperature seemed to have shifted already. He'd interrupted a convivial gathering of like-minded careerists who were hopeful of a productive networking opportunity, but had just been forced to switch off the mutual appreciation. As he crossed his legs Valentine became crudely aware of the last encounter his shoes had had with polish.

'I believe you gatecrashed our press conference, Major.' He didn't feel comfortable with first name terms so soon.

Martin spluttered a polite laugh. 'Come on, Bob, you weren't here and we needed someone with authority to head things up. Tom helped out at my behest.'

He couldn't confirm it, not just now anyway, but to his ear it sounded like Dino was altering her accent, stretching her vowels. He had certainly never heard her use a word like *behest* before. West-coast Scots were embarrassed by the way they sounded in wider company, their lack of BBC pronunciation had created the mangled, laughing-stock accents the likes of Lulu, and now Martin, adopted.

'Oh, really, you just helped us out.' The DI turned to face the major. 'Bit convenient that you happened to be in the area.'

Rutherford never got a chance to answer – Martin cut in – 'Well we're grateful he was.'

The major's thin smile seemed to linger a little too long before he spoke. 'Perhaps I should make myself scarce, until you two have had a chance to catch up.'

'That won't be necessary, will it, Bob?'

'Not at all. The Major is pretty near the top of my catch-up list right now, I wouldn't want to let the opportunity slide.'

'I've already informed your superior officer of all I'm prepared to say about our mutual interest.' The blunt, clipped tone was there to put the DI in his place.

'I don't think I made myself clear, *Tom*, this is a murder investigation that I'm conducting. The law is very clear about how we treat the act of killing in civilised society. I'm sure it's very different in a war zone, but we like to get to the bottom of things here.'

'That's enough, Bob.' The CS's old tone had returned.

'I don't believe it is, not by a long stroke. Or any kind of stroke, and that was some stroke you pulled coming down here and derailing my press conference.'

'Bob . . .'

'I'm not finished, yet. Not with Major Rutherford or with Darren Millar or James Tulloch, another Royal Highland Fusilier, though I'm sure you know that, *Tom*.'

'Right, Bob. Thank you, you can leave us the same way you came in.' Martin stood up and pointed to the door like she was directing traffic. 'I'll speak to you later, Inspector, keep your phone on. And by the way, I haven't forgotten about the divi commander's team-building exercise, I'll see you about that soon too.'

Valentine rose, nodded to the major, whose smile was now back in place, creeping up the side of his face. It didn't seem like the time for parting handshakes so Valentine tapped his brow in a mocking salute.

In the hallway the DI tried to process what he had just been part of. It was like an old-school-tie gathering that he'd worn the wrong colours to. Martin was on instinctual suck-up mode, rank always impressed her but paired to haughty arrogance like Rutherford's she was helpless. The implications for the investigation worried Valentine, neither of them could get in the way of real justice, but they could both slow it down a great deal. He didn't think Martin was stupid enough to consciously intervene, but she was vain enough to get caught up in the machinations of an old boys' network that wanted to serve its own ends. He didn't know what it was they were hiding but if he was to have any chance of discovering that – and keeping Rutherford out of his investigation – then he'd have to make it a priority.

'Christ almighty.' He removed his mobile phone, called McAlister.

'Hello, boss.'

'I take it Phil's driving?'

'Yeah, and if they ever make a *Miss Daisy 2* . . .'

'Tell him to plant the bloody foot. I want you at the barracks yesterday.'

'I presume things didn't go well with Dino?'

'When do they ever, Ally? She's surpassed herself this time, though.'

'Meaning?'

'She's cosying up to our army buddy, half expected him to get his bugle out and let her give it a spit and polish.'

'Oh aye.'

'It was not a pretty sight, let me tell you. And I can tell you this, if it continues we're going to be the ones suffering.'

'It's already an uphill struggle, boss.'

'Don't I know it. Look, I want you to get moving, we'll have to get this army angle looked into right away; who knows what kind of obstacles Rutherford will start throwing in our way if he thinks he's got Dino backing him.'

'Yes, boss.'

'And do not take any bullshit from shiny arses at the barracks, in or out of uniform.' He injected a threat into his order: 'Trust me, if you come back empty-handed I'll have you both re-posted as dog-handlers in John O'Groats!'

25

Jade Millar awoke to the sound of a newspaper being rustled by her bed. There was another sound, voices – Niall's and Darry's – that seemed to be increasing in volume. She sat up, tried to focus her gaze on the pair of them but they remained a blur. Just two bodies separated by an expanse of white paper. She rubbed her eyeballs, yawned and forced her cold feet into the trainers that sat next to the bed.

'What's going on?' she said.

'Oh, you're finally awake?' said Niall. 'This is what's going on!' He grabbed the newspaper from Darry and ran to her side of the room. 'Look, look at this.'

At first, Jade didn't want to look. She wanted to stand in the shower, get some breakfast, coffee maybe. If this was the way the day was starting then it was not a good start at all. Just what was Niall doing with a newspaper? She'd never seen him with a newspaper, never known him to read one, they were so last century.

'What am I looking at?' She took the paper, squinted. The words and pictures on the page became even more of a blur, then started to move in and out of focus.

'There!' Darry dived behind her on the bed and stuck a finger towards the page. 'Read it. Sound familiar?'

There was a picture of a group of men sitting at a desk behind nameplates and a water carafe, they looked a serious lot. As she read the caption beneath the picture she registered that they were police and something inside her chimed with recent events. A constricting panic gripped her chest.

'Oh my God.'

'Exactly,' said Darry. 'It's Jim Tulloch they're there for, you know the rest so you don't need to read on, except for the last paragraph.' Her brother rocked the bed where they sat as he got up, moved to the hallway and reached for his jacket.

Jade's stomach was starting to turn over as she read the final comments on the newspaper story, a late addition which had clearly been appended after the reporter had filed the copy. 'Mum. They've found Mum.'

Niall put an arm around her. 'She's in the hospital.'

'What, *why*? What's wrong with her?'

Darry was at the door again, fastening his jacket. 'That's what I'm going to find out.'

'But you can't,' said Jade, gripping her stomach now. 'What about me?'

'You've got Niall there, and he's got a baseball bat that nearly stoved my head in to look after you.'

Niall gripped Jade's shoulders tighter. 'We'll be fine, Darry. Go and see how your mum is.'

Darry walked towards his sister, removed his hands from his pockets and placed them on either side of her face. There were tears on her cheeks, he rubbed them away with his thumbs. 'Jade, I know it's not been easy, but it's over now, mostly. You just need to keep it together for a little while longer and then we'll be fine, just like we were before.'

She looked up. 'Before *he* came?'

Darry nodded. 'Just like before.'

'It won't be like when Dad was still here, though.' She tightened her hold on her stomach.

'No, Jade, Dad's gone but so's Tulloch. There's just you, me and Mum now.'

'And . . .' She turned to her boyfriend and flung a hand to her mouth but it wasn't enough to stem the rapid vomiting.'

'Jade,' said Niall. 'You OK?'

Darry stepped away, cleared a space for his sister to run to the bathroom. 'Let her through.'

Niall retreated to the wall, then followed after Jade. Darry held him back. 'It's all right, she's fine.'

'She's just been sick.'

'Don't worry about that. Just look after her while I'm away, Niall. Stay inside and stay away from the windows, keep the curtains drawn too. And if anyone comes to the door ignore it.'

The young lad didn't look too sure, his gaze still locked on the bathroom door. 'OK.'

'And here, take these for you and Jade.' He handed over a little plastic bag full of SIM cards. 'I have all the numbers saved into my phone, they can't trace us if we keep changing them.'

'But what about you?'

'I have a bunch of them too, we have to keep changing them, after every call. Do you understand?'

He nodded. 'I'll make sure Jade knows, too . . . Shouldn't you get going?'

Darry made a final glance around the room, as if making sure he hadn't left anything, then ran back to the bed and raised the mattress. He patted the divan with his free hand and retrieved a small package, wrapped in a ripped Tesco carrier. 'I won't leave this here with Jade the way she is.'

'What is it?' said Niall.

Darry opened the bag, removed a filthy oil cloth. Inside was a worn, black pistol.

'Christ, where did you get that?'

'I could tell you,' he raised the Luger to Niall's head, 'but I'd have to kill you.'

Niall pushed the handgun away. 'Bugger off. That's not funny. Is it loaded?'

'Don't concern yourself with that.' He tucked the pistol inside his coat and walked through the door.

It didn't seem right to be hiding away in Fin's flat, it made her feel like she was the one in trouble, but what had she done really? Jade didn't want to feel the way she did, like a criminal. Tulloch had made her feel bad enough, for long enough. He was the one that should feel bad but he couldn't feel anything now. That didn't seem right either. Tulloch was gone but they were all still suffering because of him; why should he be the one to get away from all of this?

Things would be different when Tulloch was out of their lives, surely. She should feel different, but she didn't, not really. If anything, she felt worse, she hated him more. The problem had increased, spread to more people. Darry and Niall were all wrapped up in it now, and so was her mum. She couldn't think about her mum without sobbing. It wasn't right, her mum didn't deserve any of this.

As she cried, Jade saw her mum in hospital, wired up to machines with nurses rushing around her. What had happened? Would she ever see her again? It was her fault, wasn't it? Jade accepted the blame, it was all her doing in the end. She was trapped, the flat was like a prison cell and she wanted her mum. If she was going to die she wasn't going to die in a hospital bed, with Darry watching over her. The images intensified, grew in her mind. She saw herself getting the news from Darry. 'Mum's dead . . . She asked for you, at the end . . .'

'No!'

'Jade, what's up?' Niall called from inside the bathroom.

She ran from the bedroom into the hall, yanked the main door open and ran onto the stairwell.

At the sound of the door smashing into the wall Niall ran into the hall holding a white towel round his waist, 'Jade . . . Jade . . . come back.' He ran to the window at the front of the hallway and tugged back the blind. 'Jade . . . Jade . . .' She was bolting down the street, the white soles of her trainers flashing on every step as she made off.

Niall stood at the window, staring down the street until Jade was out of view. As she disappeared he planted his wet brow on the windowpane and closed his eyes. He had only closed his eyes for a few seconds when he reopened them and found himself returning another intense gaze.

'Who the bloody hell are you?' he mouthed, trying hard

not to permit lip-reading. The man was stout, in his fifties and wearing a black leather jacket that stopped just beyond his waist. Niall looked the man up and down, black trousers and shoes too, and a black shirt. 'It's a country and western get-up, surely.'

Niall laughed as the man walked towards the building, but his amusement subsided the closer the man got. He never once let his stare drop, even as he was falling from view. When he was gone, Niall yanked his hand from the blinds and turned back to the now empty flat. He saw his wet footprints on the lino, following all the way down the hall to where he stood at the window. The main door was still open, swaying on its hinges; the sound of heavy footsteps echoed up the stairwell.

He started to shiver as a shrill blast of cold blew down the hallway. Niall cradled his chest in his arms, gripped at his elbows. Down the hall, beyond the stand where the coats hung, he saw the baseball bat but the weapon was cut from view when the door burst open. Another man, taller, younger, still in black leather but without hair stood in the open hall.

'Who're you?' said Niall.

The man didn't speak. He turned away, looked into the flat. 'You on your own?'

'I am now.'

'Where's the girl?'

'Gone.'

'Where to?'

Niall shrugged. 'She never told me. She doesn't tell me everything.'

'And you expect me to believe that? What about Fin, the owner of this flat that you're staying in, where's he?'

'I'm not sure.'

'You're not sure?'

'Not exactly. I mean, he's moving about.'

The second man strolled through the door, hands in the pockets of his jacket. 'What about my money, I take it that's on the move with him?'

'What money?'

The men stared at Niall, his thin shoulders white against the dark wall. He was still shivering. A small pool of water had gathered at his feet.

'I hope you're not going to play silly buggers with us, son.'

'Tell me what you want.'

The two men looked at each other, then turned away without speaking.

The bald man closed the door, started to remove his jacket. 'You're going to tell us where Finnie and the money are but first I'm going to have a wee bit of fun finding out.'

26

Valentine eased open the door of the incident room and called out to DS McCormack. She was seated in front of a computer, staring at the screen as she wagged a pencil beside her ear. She looked deep in thought, but snapped out of it when she heard the DI's voice.

'Sylvia, grab your coat,' said Valentine. 'And can you grab mine for me too?' He let the door swing closed and as he was turning, a rushing DI Harris halted in his stride and put out a hand. 'How goes it, Bob?'

The detective's expression, especially the glowering gaze, said it all. 'Do you really want an answer to that, Eddy?'

'Probably not, judging by the kip of you.' He placed a palm flat on the wall, exposing a chunky gold watch. 'Not got the building blocks down on the murder case, then?'

'Not got the blocks delivered, yet.'

Harris drummed fingers on the wall, the watch rattled in accompaniment. 'I was hoping to grab five minutes with you.'

'Not now Eddy, I have the victim's partner in Ayr Hospital just coming round after a hit and run.'

'Oh, yeah, the scrambler on the High Street. Another daft wee boy racer who's going to find himself in more grief than he bargained for.'

'He'll not be playing Kick Start in this town again, put it that way. Look, what were you after anyway?' He glanced into the office, McCormack was picking up his jacket, folding it over her arm.

'Norrie Leask, some very strange goings on with him at the moment.'

'Really? Is there another kind of goings on with that nut-job?'

Harris eased away from the wall and smoothed the edges of his moustache, as if he was trying to affect a more serious look. 'Even by Leask's standards he's hyper. You might say, jumpy.'

'Go on.'

'Has been rattling a lot of cages in the town, putting the big threat about here and there, which in itself isn't unusual for Leask but nobody's saying why, and that is unusual.'

Valentine listened to the DI but was puzzled why the normally cagey Harris was being so open with the details of his case. 'There's been a crime, a serious one. Nobody wants to be involved, that's how it works,' said Valentine; he retrieved his coat from McCormack as she appeared in the hallway.

'Who are we talking about?' said McCormack.

'Norrie Leask. Local psycho-cum-club owner. Runs a place called the Meat Hangers.'

The DS's expression altered, she pointed back to the incident room. 'I've just been reading about that place on James Tulloch's file.'

Harris switched his attention from Valentine to McCormack. 'Isn't Tulloch your victim?'

'Yes, he's ex-army,' said McCormack, 'but he was working

as a jumped-up bouncer recently, some sort of nightclub security. I'm sure the file said he was employed at the Meat Hangers.'

Valentine pushed open the office door, stamped back towards the PC that McCormack had just been sitting at. He started to scroll down the screen. 'Where did you see this, Sylvia?'

'Just there!' she pointed on the screen. 'Yeah, there it is . . . Employer name, Leask, Meat Hangers nightclub.'

Harris had joined them. 'Jesus . . .'

'He's not going to help Norrie Leask when I get hold of him.'

'We should bring him in, sir,' said McCormack. 'See if he feels talkative.'

'I know where he is,' said Harris. 'We've been keeping a shadow on him temporarily.'

'Only temporary?'

'You know how Dino is with budgets just now, Bob. We could only follow his movements in office hours, there's no time-and-a-half going this weather, especially when we don't have anything on him.'

Valentine shook his head. 'We should ask the scroats just to commit crimes nine-to-five, that would make life so much easier for us.'

Harris turned away from the officers, headed back down the hall to his own office. 'Look, I'll bring Leask in. I'll let you know when we have him and if you want to sit in that's fine with me.'

'Do that, Eddy. If Leask's tied up in this I'll have him on a platter.'

147

'You'll get in line behind me, mate, slight matter of the armed robbery to solve too.'

Valentine watched as DI Harris padded away from the incident room, but his thoughts were on the night of James Tulloch's murder. A lot of money had gone missing from Leask's club in the raid and that amount of cash was a strong motive for murder. If the two incidents were linked then perhaps the pieces of the puzzle would slide together more easily than he thought. Just why Flash Harris was being so helpful was more worrying. It wasn't his style, unless there was something in it for him too.

'What do you think, Sylvia?' he said.

'I think we've very little else to go on. Is Leask capable?'

'That I don't know. He's a tin-pot hard man but murder would be stepping up a few leagues, even for him.'

'If the money was the issue, well, a lot of heads have been turned for a few quid.'

'But, presumably the money was Leask's, it was from his club.'

'He'd want it back, surely.'

'So he's angry enough to kill for it, maybe. I'd be more inclined to see Leask as a profiteer, but he'd certainly be daft enough to get involved in murder if his cut was big enough.'

'But where does Tulloch come in, has he robbed his cut, sir?' said McCormack.

'There was no sign of money at the scene, only a victim's corpse. Of course, if Tulloch copped it for the cash, there would be no sign of the cash or the killer.'

'They'd both be long gone.'

Valentine slotted his arms into his pinstripe jacket. 'It's an interesting scenario.'

'We should certainly kick over Leask's skittles.'

'Don't worry about that, Eddy's getting into his bovver boots as we speak. Meanwhile, nothing's altered enough to derail us, we need to question Sandra Millar. If anyone's likely to throw some light on Tulloch's murder it's her.'

'Agnes Gilchrist puts her at the scene at just the right time, she knows something that's for sure.'

Valentine started to descend the stairs. 'Let's hope she gives it up nicely. I'd hate to have to borrow Eddy's boots myself.'

27

The meeting with the chief super and Major Rutherford had soured Valentine's mood. He had not been particularly cheerful before, was not even in the vicinity, but now an angry rook was pecking at his mind. There would be more to come, CS Martin had been undermined, and to make matters worse, in front of someone she clearly had a need to impress. It didn't matter whether she was taken with Rutherford's accent and old-school-tie bonhomie or just the cut of his jib, the result would be the same. Valentine saw the case slipping away from him, he was losing control.

'Here, you drive, Sylvia.' He handed over the car keys.

'Yes, sir.'

Valentine rarely let anyone drive his car but he needed time to think. As he got in the passenger's side he found there was no space for his legs. He wanted to stretch out, but as he pushed his back into the fixed seat he groaned. 'Bloody hell . . .'

'All OK, sir?'

'How do you put this back a bit?'

'There's a wee bar that you press. It's under the seat, sir.'

Valentine fumbled for the lever. 'Where about?'

'Here, let me.'

As Sylvia reached under the seat to release the chair

Valentine looked away, scanned the car park. There was no one there. 'Good job Ally and Phil never saw that.'

'What do you mean?'

'They think we're on.'

'*On*, sir?'

'It must be an Ayrshire expression. They think we're getting a bit close, spending too much time together.'

'Oh for God's sake. It's only the nature of the case, they should realise I have experience of this sort of crime from Glasgow.'

'Well if they don't they better get used to it. I can see all of us burning the midnight oil from here on.' He fastened his seatbelt. 'Look, I meant to say, about the other day with Crosbie, thanks for that.'

'No bother, only trying to help.'

Valentine played with a cuff-button and watched the road ahead as they approached the King Street roundabout. 'Well, there's help and there's help. That sort of thing's well above the call of duty.'

'Most of what I do is,' she grinned to herself.

Valentine gave a knowing nod. 'I don't know if it was the meeting with Crosbie or what, but I've not had any funny turns since.'

'Is that what you're calling them now?'

'Seems to fit. Mind you, the way this case is going I could do with the help.'

DS McCormack glanced in the rear-view mirror and pulled onto the bypass, the car started to accelerate. 'Well, we have Sandra Millar now and this Leask lead could be promising.'

'Promising for who, us or Eddy Harris? I don't trust him and the way things are shaping up Dino's likely to put me out to grass and hand the lot over to Harris.'

'She wouldn't do that.'

'Wouldn't she? I've seen her tricks first-hand and she's capable of a lot worse, let me tell you.'

'But Harris isn't as senior an officer as you, doesn't have as much experience. She wouldn't dare.'

'Trust me, if these cases are linked then it's a possibility. We need to be ahead of the game, ahead of bloody Flash Harris.'

'I'll get a hold of the case files from the Meat Hangers robbery when we're done at the hospital. I'll go over them tonight.'

Valentine tapped his fingers on the rim of the window-ledge, a smattering of rain had started to fall making the grim Ayrshire setting seem worse than usual. 'The robbery was on the same night and our victim worked there; if we have Tulloch at the club earlier in the evening then that's something for us to go on. What's Leask saying about Tulloch's death, has he got previous form with him that might tempt theft? You'll have to dig for any animosity because I presume it won't be obvious or Leask'd have just given him his jotters.'

'I'll visit the club and sniff around the staff. I'd suggest a covert visit but I don't think we've got the time to set that up, sir.'

'Just brass it out. Go in heavy, get the complete personnel list and run them all through the system. If there's any with convictions for violence, run them through the mincer. If there was bad blood between Tulloch and anyone, even in small amounts, I want to know about it.'

'Yes, sir.'

The detective dropped his voice, took a more contemplative tone. 'Just bear one thing in mind, Sylvia, if we end up sharing an incident room with Eddy Harris the only way we're going to keep the good biccies on our side of the table is by making him look like an absolute bloody muppet.'

Darkness had fallen by the time the detectives reached the hospital. A queue of vehicles waited to enter the car park, their disgruntled drivers watching in disbelief as DI Valentine pointed McCormack into the emergency bays at the front of the building.

'Are you sure about this?' said the DS.

'It's an emergency isn't it?'

'Well . . .'

'Sylvia, if murder isn't an emergency then what is?' She didn't look convinced. 'And anyway, who's going to ticket a DI?'

'Point taken.'

They headed for the front door of the large, well-lit building. The hospital had not been there long, was close enough in recent memory for Valentine to remember when it was still farmland, but the exterior looked worn and weather-beaten already. Peeling paint and sun-faded window frames highlighted by bright spotlighting. Inside, the reception desk was through a further set of automatic doors, a blonde-wood facia – there seemed to be a design theme – covered the wall either side of the corridor.

'When did hospitals start to look like branches of Ikea?' said Valentine.

'I've no idea, sir. But they do now.'

'Bet you wish you'd bought those shares in allen keys, eh?'

The receptionist pointed the detectives to the lift and said she would ring ahead to the ward to let them know the police had arrived. She was balancing the receiver on her shoulder, speaking in an unnatural volume to rise above the clamour of voices around the desk, as they left her. On the third floor, more blinding light and a powerful antiseptic smell greeted the officers. Valentine got as far as the middle of the long corridor, following the numbers on doors, before he stopped still.

'Where's our uniforms?' he said.

'There doesn't appear to be any here.'

'That's what I mean. There should be. Ally should have had one on the door, this is a bloody murder suspect.'

McCormack looked the length of the hallway and back again. 'Maybe he tried to put someone on but was overruled.'

'I don't think so, Sylvia,' Valentine looked through raised lids, 'unless Dino's opened a rolling expenses spreadsheet for this case alone.'

'I wouldn't put it past her.'

'No, neither would I. But I'll give her the benefit of the doubt on this occasion, given that she's been otherwise engaged all day with her new major friend.'

'I'll check it out, sir.' McCormack removed a notebook from her bag and started to scribble.

'Do that. And make sure it's round-the-clock surveillance,

I don't want Sandra Millar left alone when she's already got a habit of going walkabout.'

As they reached the door to the patient's room a man in a short-sleeved shirt, a lanyard with an ID badge around his neck flapping, started to jog to meet them. 'Hello, you must be the police officers.'

'You must be the doctor?' said Valentine.

He tapped the badge round his neck. 'No getting anything past you – Ben Caruthers.'

'Shall we go inside, Doctor?'

'Before we do, can I just say, she's not in the best condition.'

McCormack returned the notebook to her bag, said, 'I thought she was lucid now.'

'I don't know if I'd use quite that term. She's conscious, but she's very confused.'

'What are you trying to say, Doctor?' said Valentine, sensing a note of over-caution from the doctor.

'I suppose what I'm trying to say is that this woman has been through a serious trauma.'

'She was knocked over by a kid on a scrambler, not a double-decker bus. And he was hardly up to ninety in the pedestrianised area of the High Street.'

'I'm not talking about the accident, Inspector. I mean Sandra Millar is suffering from pronounced anxiety, she's under a serious amount of stress and confusion. Her nerves are bad, she blacks out and she's got memory loss.'

'That's convenient,' said Valentine. 'Have you any idea how many murder suspects I interview with memory loss, Doctor?'

'I don't mean to make it sound like she's affecting these symptoms, she's really not well. She's likely to be suffering some form of post-traumatic stress, that's a fragile state for anyone to be in. I'm merely asking you to be considerate of that.'

Valentine turned for the door, grabbed the handle, 'I'll bear that in mind, Doctor.'

As the DI opened the door a flat-screen television, suspended on a bracket above the bed, was the only source of light. He flicked the switch on the wall and illuminated the whole room. A huddled mass, curled in the middle of the bed, recoiled.

'It's all right, Sandra, you can catch up with the *Hollyoaks* omnibus on Sunday,' said Valentine. He walked to the bedside, where he was joined by DS McCormack. Dr Caruthers moved to the other side of the bed and tried to settle his patient. As Sandra jerked upright in the bed her gaze darted between the two officers and the doctor who examined the catheter on the back of her hand.

Valentine was unmoved, he reached over Sandra and retrieved the remote control, flicked off.

'I hear you've lost your memory, Sandra?'

'Have I?' her voice was a whisper.

'Very good, of course you wouldn't remember that either.' He put his hands in his pockets. 'Where have you been, my dear?'

'I don't know what you mean?'

'Since James Tulloch was murdered in your kitchen, Sandra.'

'Who?'

'Oh, I see. You're going to claim you don't remember your boyfriend, now.'

Her face was impassive. Dark circles sat under her eyes, just above drawn cheeks and the straight, thin line of her mouth. 'I remember Jade.'

DS McCormack spoke: 'Where is Jade?'

'I don't know. I want to see her. She's my daughter.'

'But she's missing, Sandra,' said Valentine. 'Just like you were until we found you rolling about on the High Street this morning. Yes, Jade's missing. And Darry, your son . . .'

The officers looked for life in her eyes but nothing showed. The talk seemed to have stilled her nerves, she sat solidly in the bed and didn't move.

'I said *Darry*, do you remember him?'

'I . . . I . . .'

Dr Caruthers intervened. 'I think you're confusing her. Perhaps if you eased off a little.'

'This is a murder investigation, a man's been stabbed to death . . . In her kitchen.'

Sandra's face contorted, the thin mouth widened and she started to whine.

'I think she's had enough now,' said the doctor.

Valentine's voice rose. 'I'll decide when she's had enough.'

'No. Actually, Inspector, that decision is mine and I think my patient has had quite enough questions for one day.'

Sandra sunk into her pillow, sobbed into the bedclothes as Dr Caruthers tried to coax her to take a sip of water. The detectives watched, McCormack nodding towards the door; when Valentine's eyes met hers he shook his head and continued with the questioning.

'We have the knife, Sandra,' said Valentine. 'And footage of you throwing it in the river, what have you got to say about that?'

She mumbled, 'Jade. I want my daughter. I want Jade. She needs me. I'm all she's got . . .'

'That's right, her father's dead too isn't he? You remember that bit OK.'

Dr Caruthers put down the glass of water and stepped towards the officers. 'That's enough now! You can see the effect your questioning's having on her. I won't watch her take a complete breakdown tonight, it's time for you both to leave. Now.'

28

It had been a day to forget for DI Bob Valentine. From the less than enthusiastic report the Glasgow boffins delivered to the encounter with Dino – and the realisation that she was more attached to the idea of sucking up to Major Rutherford than helping the case – things could hardly get worse. Sandra Millar turning up should have improved matters, but after visiting her in hospital it was obvious that she couldn't be of any use to the investigation. She was clearly not well; even if she admitted to the murder the chances of the fiscal taking it on were doubtful without some forensic evidence too. If it did go to court the defence would have the stronger case. It would be one more thing for Dino to use against him, and the attendant bad publicity would be yielded like a lash on the force. And anyway, Valentine wasn't convinced that Sandra Millar was the killing type.

He had met many like her before. Demure, hard-done-by women who had snapped after a lifetime of beatings and brutality. Men weren't immune either, he'd encountered the disorder in both sexes. The usual MO seemed to be that they took the abuse for years, listened to the belittling voice for so long that they believed it, and then almost in spite of themselves some animal instinct arrived and they attacked.

It was as if human beings were only able to take so much torture before their programming, or was it just a preference, to fight took over. He'd seen a Kilmarnock woman from way back who had lasted to her seventieth year before spiking her husband's morning coffee with paraquat then casually calling in the police. She said she had never had such a good night's sleep afterwards; her conscience was intact. That wasn't the case with Sandra Millar, she was bothered by something, but what? It was against his experience for someone like her to kill and then crack, normally it was the other way about. Sandra was deep in guilt about Tulloch's murder, and that confused the DI.

As Valentine put the key in the door to his home he was surprised to see a light still on in the living room. It wouldn't be Clare, surely; she would have went to bed long ago. As he stepped inside his curiosity subsided as he found his father nodding into sleep in the armchair.

'Still up, Dad?' he said.

His father's head jerked upright. 'Och, just about. I've been dozing off for the last wee while.' He sat up, put the picture he was holding on the arm of the chair; the action seemed to spark his memory. 'I called you at work today.'

'I saw that, sorry I meant to call back.'

'Not at all,' he interrupted. 'I thought it was a silly enough thing for me to be calling you. I didn't disturb you or get you into bother did I?'

Valentine found the suggestion, after all of today's troubles, mildly humorous. 'No, Dad, it's fine.'

'It was this, you realise.' He held up the picture that had been drawn by Hugh Crosbie. 'What a likeness, it is.'

The detective put his briefcase on the floor and started to remove his jacket. He hadn't expected a response to the picture, he didn't really know what he expected to come of it when he took it home. 'You recognise him?'

'Aye, well, I was going to say he's . . .' The old man cut himself off, started to rise from the chair. 'Hear, you'll want to grab your tea. Clare has something in the fridge on a plate, do you want me to heat it in the microwave?'

Valentine waved his father back down, impatience building, said, 'Just be at peace would you? I'll grab a bit of cheese on toast.'

'Give you nightmares, at this time of night.'

'Can they be worse than the ones I have during the day? Look, who's this in the picture, Dad, are you going to tell me?'

'It's Bert.' His father blurted out the name like it should have some meaning.

'Who?'

'Och, you'll not know him. It's Bert McCrindle, no doubt about it, he was your mother's cousin.'

'He looks before my time right enough.' Valentine removed the picture from the arm of the chair. 'A military man?'

'Not really, that's him on his National Service. He was in the war right enough, out in the deserts of Africa, never talked about it, don't think it was an experience we'd understand.'

'Well you wouldn't talk about it, especially if it was traumatic.'

His father nodded once and then turned away, seemingly

161

mulling the thought over. His heavily lined face started to droop, lose some creases. 'He was a prisoner of war, y'know. I didn't know that until your mother told me, it made sense of a lot for me, he was always a funny bloke. I remember one Christmas being at his place dropping off coal, he was in the back garden and we saw this wee rat, just one and nothing special, not like a pit rat, but it rattled him. I'd never seen a man turn so white, the life drained away from him.'

'So he didn't like rats, I'm not a fan myself.'

'It wasn't that, son. Your mother told me, when he was a prisoner, they dug giant pits and caged them in, in the ground like, the rats used to run along the top on the wires . . . it never left him. He was bothered something terrible with his nerves afterwards, always was the whole time I knew him.'

'In some ways, I'm sure, it was as bad as shell shock. There's a lot goes on in war that we can't imagine, I'm sure.'

His father was shaking his head. 'No, it's not that. Something else. There was some kind of incident that he endured, I don't know what it was I can only imagine. Your mother spoke about it once and then she regretted it, saw it as a betrayal to Bert, and I never pressed her on it because it wasn't something I had any right to know.'

'But we can surmise from Mam's reaction that it damaged him in some way.'

'That we can.' He turned to face his son, widening his gaze. 'But the picture, why have you got a pencil drawing of Bert on the fridge? That's what I want to know.'

Valentine exhaled slowly, a rational response was impossible to find. 'You wouldn't believe me.'

'Try me.'

'OK. Let me rephrase that, you wouldn't want to know.'

'I've already said I want to know, now will you stop beating about the bush and tell me.'

'Well, don't say I didn't warn you.' Valentine loosened the knot on his tie, pulled it through the collar and started to roll it around his fist. 'A colleague of mine had worked with what you might call a medium, someone who helps police with their enquiries by, I don't know what you'd call it, supernatural means.'

His father stared intently. 'Yes, yes. I quite understand.'

'And, well, long story short is that this medium, a chappie called Hugh, drew the picture.' He looked at his father again, wanted to make sure he hadn't changed his opinion after finding out more. 'It's what he does – when he sees spirits he draws them and passes on their pictures to the people he believes they're trying to communicate with.'

'In the name of God.' His father's eyes sunk back in his head, he turned away. 'I cannot think for the life of me why old Bert would have been trying to communicate with you, Bob. I mean, the mind just boggles.'

Valentine finished rolling up his tie, rose, and walked for the kitchen door. 'You're not alone in that assessment, Dad. But I'm routinely stunned if anything that happens to me makes any sense.'

'Are you off to get that bite?'

'I am.'

'Well, sorry to add to your woes, but I finished the cheese.'

163

29

As the young man turned the corner he stopped still, stood facing DI Bob Valentine. For a moment the detective stared, who was he? There was a hint of recognition but nothing he could be sure of. As he took two more steps, drew nearer, the man spoke. 'Bob, we've never met but I feel I know you.'

'I don't think so.' He sidestepped, moved around the man.

'No, don't go.'

A hand grabbed Valentine's arm, his coat sleeve was tugged. 'What are you doing?'

'You can't go.' The man tightened his grip.

'You realise I'm a police officer.'

This seemed to provoke hilarity in the man, 'Of course. There would be no point in my stopping you in the street otherwise. I have important information about the death of the fusilier . . . James Tulloch.'

Valentine brushed away the man's hand. 'I never released that information.'

'I never said you did. Look, I know lots of things that aren't public knowledge, can we talk, Bob?'

Valentine didn't like the familiarity of first names, he was toying with the idea of arresting the man, taking him to King Street and picking over the information he seemed so free with. He looked around, it was Alloway Street, outside the Arnotts department store, the name had changed but the store would always be Arnotts to anyone with history in Ayr. The town was quiet, beyond quiet – they were the only ones around. He asked himself what time of the day it was and found he couldn't reply.

'Do I know you, son?'

A laugh. He opened his hand and led him into the store. They took the elevator to the cafe, they were the only people there. The absence of anyone else unsettled Valentine but he found himself going along with it, not through curiosity, but because he was powerless to do anything else.

'You look a bit confused, Bob.'

'Where is everyone?'

'Not here.' The man sat down, removed his overcoat and hung it on the chair. 'And before you ask, here's not where you think it is.'

He recognised the man now, the uniform he wore underneath his coat. 'You're Bert, the one my dad was talking about.' His vision blurred, his head ached. 'The hell's going on here?'

'Don't ask me questions, Bob. Just listen.'

'This is insane. Something's not right . . .'

Bert followed the detective's line of vision, brushed the buttons on his chest. 'You're looking for a soldier.'

'*What*?'

'And you're looking for a lad that's missing, but he's already dead.'

Valentine's hands started to sweat, he put them under the table. 'How do you know this?'

165

'I just do. And you need to trust me because you've no one else. Now listen, find the soldier, he knows what this is about. If you don't find him there'll only be more blood.'

He shook his head. 'Have you any idea how hard this is for me to believe? I saw a picture of you but you've never existed for me.'

'Am I not real enough, Bob?'

'Jesus Christ, you're asking me that? I don't know if I'm real enough.'

'I think you know what I'm telling you is real. Find the soldier, he needs help, I know what he's been through and he can't handle it on his own.'

Bert stood up, collected his coat and draped it over his arm. 'I'm off now, I don't think there's much chance of a waitress in here.'

'And where's here? It's not bloody well Arnotts.'

'No, it's more of a halfway house.' He looked around him. 'Go on then, don't waste what I've given you.'

'Wait. You said there was a missing boy, we don't have a missing boy on this case.'

'But you will. Goodbye, Bob.' The voice changed as the detective's name was uttered.

'No. Wait . . .'

'Bob,' someone else was calling him. 'Be quiet. You'll wake the girls.' It was Clare. She sat over him in bed, reached for the light. 'You're sweating, you were shouting in your sleep.'

Valentine raised himself on the bed, his heart pounding. 'I'm sorry.'

166

Clare's cold hand touched his shoulder. 'Are you all right?'

'No, I'm losing the plot . . .'

'What?'

He got out of bed and stumbled to the bathroom, the bright lights stung his eyes. He leaned over the sink clutching his chest and started to splash water on his face and neck.

'Bob, what's going on?' She followed him into the bathroom. 'You're as white as a maggot, you look like . . .'

'Like I've seen a ghost.'

'I was going to say like you're having a heart attack.'

'That sounds preferable.' He tried to fill a glass of water but his hands were trembling too much.

Clare took the glass, filled it and held the water to his mouth. 'You need to calm yourself.'

'Easier said than done.'

'Come back to bed, try to get some sleep. I'm sure things will look better in the morning.'

'Sleep, are you kidding me?' He pushed away the glass and staggered back to the bedroom, sat on the edge of the bed. The flesh on his arms was pimpling, he slapped his palms together.

Clare followed him through. 'Should I call a doctor?'

'Maybe. Is there a psychiatrist on call at this time?'

'I don't follow . . .'

'It all seemed so real.'

'What did?'

'I was there, I mean like the last time . . . with the Janie Cooper case.'

'That was the little girl that went missing, wasn't it?'

167

'Everywhere, I saw her everywhere. Christ above, if this is a rerun of that, I don't think I can stand it, Clare.'

'The dreams again? The visions, that's what this is about?'

Valentine rose and started to pace the room. He needed to talk, to tell someone what he'd been going through. He relayed the story about the man in the hospital room when Agnes Gilchrist died and the visit to Hugh Crosbie.

'Who's Sylvia?' said Clare.

'My DS . . . Why do you ask that?'

'And why is she taking a special interest in your problems?'

'Are you seriously making a thing of this?'

'I'm just asking, because I would have thought your first port of call might have been your wife.'

Valentine raised his hands. 'I've just told you everything.'

'But you told her first.'

'Yes. She has experience, she's worked with precognitives before. It was Sylvia who put me in touch with Crosbie.'

Clare moved from the bed to the other side of the room and started to remove her dressing gown. As she turned back towards Valentine she stared briefly then slit her eyes towards the bedside lamp. She didn't return her gaze as she got into bed and switched out the light.

30

Jade stood in the darkness beyond the hospital car park, just far enough into the copse of trees to be able to see lights burning in the building. The rain had stopped but some drops clinging to the leaves above her managed to dislodge themselves and fall on her. She looked up, towards the pale moon, and the cold night's wind touched her face.

She tried not to think about Niall, about the way she had left the flat, but his voice seemed to be following her. He would be OK, he would get over her running off like that, and anyway, it wasn't his battle to fight. She'd decided that the moment Niall went for Darry with the bat. Her brother had so effortlessly disarmed him, pushed him to the ground, that it was obvious to her Niall was out of his depth. He was a nice boy, a good friend to have and she had needed him once but not now.

Jade didn't need to use Niall as cover anymore, she had passed the point where it mattered if her mother or brother found out the truth.

'Jade . . . Jade, where are you?' It was Darry.

'Over here.' She rushed to the fence at the edge of the car park, the grass was long and wet and slowed her movement.

'God, you're soaking wet, girl.'

'It's been raining.' She pushed back her wet fringe. 'Did you see Mum?'

'Of course I did.' Darry leant a hand over the fence and helped his sister to climb up. She stumbled at the top wire and he lifted her down. He looked into the field behind her. 'Where's Niall?'

'He's not coming.'

'What?'

'It's nothing to do with him, Darry.'

'But he was supposed to be helping you.'

She raised her eyebrows to the sky. 'He's just a boy, he can barely look after himself.'

'Jade, is everything OK? You don't look well.' He placed a hand on her arm; Jade knocked it away.

'I'm fine. Just wet that's all.'

'Have you been sick again?'

'No, I'm fine I just told you.' She started to step away from her brother, 'Are you coming or are we staying out in the cold and wet all night?'

Darry ran after her. 'Wait. We can't go in there.'

'I thought you said I could go and see her, once you came back.'

'Not now. There's police in there now.'

'Police? . . . Why are the police in there?'

Darry tried to steer his sister away from the conspicuously lit hospital. 'Come on, we'll get a taxi out of here.'

'No. I want to see Mum.' She yanked her arm away and started back towards the hospital.

'Jade, that's not going to be possible. That copper was fuming, in a minute or two the place is going to be crawling with police. Now come on, we need to get going or we'll be locked up.'

'We haven't done anything.' She struggled with her brother, a woman in a blue Corsa rolled down her window and stared over.

'Jade, you're making a scene. Calm down.'

'I want to see Mum, you're hurting my arm.'

'Jade, I mean it. We need to get out of here.'

Her voice rose, 'Why? What have *we* done? Why are the police with Mum?'

'Jade, I'm supposed to be in barracks. They'll break my bloody legs for this.'

Darry's mention of the army stopped his sister's struggling. He'd risked a lot for her and he saw that she understood that. 'They think she did it, don't they? The police think Mum killed him.'

Norrie Leask leaned onto the dashboard and pointed to the turn-off, 'Here, Joe, take this one.'

'You sure now?'

'They all look the bloody same to me, especially in the dark.'

'Cumnock countryside's a black hole in the daylight as well.'

'Those miners must have wanted to stay underground, bloody shite-hole.' The car shuddered on the uneven track, slowed by a shallow trench and scattered gravel. 'Aye, this is the spot. That's the milestone for the old road pithead, there.'

'You sure no one ever comes out this way?'

Leask put another hand on the dash, steadied himself as the track got bumpier. 'Are you kidding me? Why would anyone come out here? It's an abandoned pit. Fraught with danger these places, we could be taking our lives in our hands just driving up here.'

Joe fired him a glower. 'Now you tell me.'

'Look, it's like this, if you want to keep him in the boot, stinking out your car and marking a big pointy finger to plod then be my guest. Me, I'd sooner not do time for this wee arsewipe.'

The car halted abruptly. Joe yanked on the handbrake and flicked his cigarette through the open window. 'Right, that's it. We can see the pithead from here. We'll carry him.'

'We? Who pays your bloody wages?'

Joe released the lock and pushed open the door. 'I don't remember that bit in my contract about disposing of dead bodies in the night, remind me about that, time-and-a-half is it?'

'Aye, that'll be right.' Leask exited on his side of the car. 'I want a pint out of you for this, mind.'

The pair walked around to the rear of the vehicle, their shoes sunk into the wet earth. Neither carried a flashlight, the only illumination came from the car's headlights. As he opened the boot Joe stared into the deep space, located the white-skinned features of Niall. The body was an inconvenience, it might once have been alive – a human being – but the connection had been lost. 'Just looks like he's sleeping, there.'

'He does as well.' Leask, turned his head to the side, squinted. 'Doesn't look too bothered about it all.'

'He was bothered when I had the pliers on his fingernails.'

'That's what I mean, the boot of a car's an improvement on his last few hours. Christ, are we going sentimental here? Let's get the wee shite in the ground. He's served his purpose.'

The two men reached in, grabbed arms and legs and lifted Niall's body from the car, in one clean heave.

'There's nothing to him,' said Joe.

'Well his mammy's meat pies will not save him now.' He nodded towards the pit-face. 'This way.'

They walked a few yards, the wet ground sinking beneath them. Joe's foot became trapped in a mud-hole, his knee headed skyward as he yanked his foot out. 'I'm just waiting for this ground to open up and swallow us. Can we not just dump him?'

'No. He's going down the shaft. Are you stupid?'

'But if nobody ever comes here, who's going to see him?' Joe lost his footing again on the uneven surface. 'Look, that's nearly another shoe away. They're Timberland you know, hundred pounds a pair.'

A little rain started to smatter their faces. 'Oh, that's all we need. I'm away back to the car.' Leask dropped his end of the load.

'Hey . . . no way.'

'Get that dumped in the pit and hurry up about it. I'm not wading through this in the rain, I pay you more than enough to manage on your own. Now, move it.'

Big Joe watched as Leask shuffled back towards the glow of the car's headlights, pushing up his collar and cursing. He lifted Niall's limp frame onto his shoulder and turned for the pit-face.

173

31

The sight of Chief Superintendent Marion Martin in the incident room was a bad enough shock to Valentine but at such an early hour he didn't need to be a detective to know something was seriously wrong. She seemed to be going over the case files, at least, that's how it looked to him as he walked, slowly and silently, towards the desk where she was sitting. She never looked up once but seemed to sense his arrival at her side, greeting him with a brusque order to grab a seat.

'I'm not stopping,' said Valentine.

The chief super looked up. 'You sound fairly confident of that, Bob. If I were standing in your boots, I'm not sure I'd be so cocksure.'

He peered beyond her towards the desk, she was indeed going over the case files – his own annotated file from inside his desk. Had she searched his office?

'If you're unhappy with the way the case is being conducted then perhaps you might want to let me get on with it so that I can contribute to your clean-up rate.'

She slammed the folder shut, tapped red fingernails on the top and eyed the detective through heavy lids. 'You're not the only DI in King Street.' She rose. 'I could replace you, like that . . .' Her fingers snapped in Valentine's face.

'Is this a conversation I should be having with the union rep present, chief?'

'You could bring along the Prime Minister, Bob, it won't make a blind bit of difference to what I have to say.' The castors on her chair squealed as she stepped back from the desk, the chair skidded into the centre of the floor. 'I'll see you in my office in ten minutes. Bring any and every scrap of progress you've made because I'll need to be convinced you are the most capable officer to handle this case.'

He knew she was testing him, asserting her rank. He knew, also, that he was about to pay for having challenged her authority too many times lately. The meeting with Major Rutherford, likely, being the offence which caused the most damage. The absurdity of the situation was annoying enough, but the pettiness bit even deeper.

'I do have other things to do,' he said.

'No, Bob. You have nothing else to do, other than what I tell you.' She crossed her arms, leaned in, 'And you can call this a wee heads-up – you might want to explain away why I have a complaint on my desk from Ayr Hospital to add to the one from the hospital in Kilmarnock. And while you're at it, just when were you going to tell me about this?' She reached into the file and retrieved the post-mortem report on James Tulloch. 'I found an extra page in your file that wasn't in mine and it says Tulloch's spinal column was cut, how did they put it? *The wound track, back to front was administered on a horizontal thrust* . . . That's pretty cleanly and coldly, like he was sitting on the bloody butcher's block.'

'I had every intention of . . .'

She raised a hand. 'Save it, Bob. My office in ten minutes.'

DS McCormack was the first of the team to arrive after Valentine, almost bumping into the chief super as they met at the doorway. The DS made for the glassed-off office at the back of the incident room where Valentine had stationed himself. He spotted her on the way in, waved her away, but she took no notice.

'Who stole your toffee?' were the first words out of her mouth.

'Is that Glasgow? This isn't the *Francie and Josie* Show, you know.'

'Sometimes I think the only folk in this country who like Glasgow are the Glaswegians.'

'You could substitute country for planet and not be far wrong.'

McCormack closed the door behind her. 'Well somebody got up on the wrong side of the bed.'

'I'm sorry. Had a rough night. Then Dino was in here early doors and it wasn't to sing me "That's Amore".'

'Erm, I'll start with the rough night, I think . . .'

Valentine pushed out his hands, inflated his chest and began a slow exhalation. He started to talk about the picture that Hugh Crosbie had drawn and then he found himself relaying his father's explanation of how he knew Bert McCrindle and how strange it all seemed to him, but by the time he got to the bit about his dream, and the visit from Bert, strange didn't seem like a strong enough description. The DI's head was heavy, bulging with new thoughts, questions, what-ifs.

'Did you tell Clare?' said McCormack.

'How could I not? She was right next to me, got the brunt

of my ranting and raving again . . . anyway, I don't want to talk about Clare just now.'

'OK. Do you want to talk about the chief super?'

'God no. That's not a choice I have though, the way she feels about me you might be the lead detective on this case soon.'

'What do you mean?'

'I'll be lucky to get a job cleaning up after the mounted police outside Ibrox if she chooses to let rip.'

'I take it she found out about the post-mortem report on Tulloch.'

'Bingo.' Valentine leaned back in his chair, turned his arms behind his neck. 'There's more too, but I won't bother you with it right now. Tell me about Phil and Ally's trip to the far east.'

'Oh, interesting, to say the least. They spoke to the top brass there, but got zilch. Pleasantries, the good biccies brought out but nothing to write home about.'

'Well, I wasn't expecting a smoking gun, Sylvia. Tell me they dug a little deeper.'

'Yes, of course, there's more.' She approached the desk, a note of optimism rising in her voice. 'They spoke to some squaddies, they knew Tulloch and didn't sound too fussed to hear he'd died. They were a bit more concerned about Darren Millar's disappearance, that's really put the cat amongst the pigeons at the barracks.'

'Darren was much more popular, then?'

'For sure. But get this, there's more. His best friend in the regiment was a bloke called Finnie, who came from, guess where? Ayr.'

'Why do I know that name?' said Valentine.

'Probably because you've seen it on Flash Harris's case files – Finnie worked at the Meat Hangers with Tulloch and they were both in the Royal Highland Fusiliers together.'

'Jesus, tell me you've pulled this Finnie in.'

McCormack shook her head. 'No, sir. He's top of Harris's list at the moment too. Apparently Finnie's not been seen since the night of the robbery.'

'And the night of the murder too, don't forget that, Sylvia.' Valentine picked up a pencil and started to roll it between his fingers. 'Has Harris pulled in Norrie Leask yet?'

'No. That's the not-so-good news: Leask's missing.'

'What do you mean missing?'

'Nowhere to be found, sir. Not at his address or known haunts, and no one has seen hide nor hair of him.'

'Well that's bloody convenient.' Valentine thrust the pencil down on the desk. 'Just what the hell is going on here? I've got a murdered ex-squaddie, a missing ex-squaddie – make that two of them missing including this Finnie character – and now Ayr's answer to Arthur Daley and Terry McCann rolled into one has done a bunk.'

McCormack squinted. 'I think it's still progress.'

Valentine wasn't so sure, he checked his watch, his ten minutes were up and he had to go and see the chief super. 'Where's Phil and Ally got to? They should be here by now.'

'They're still on the east coast, sir.'

'You're joking?'

'They stopped overnight, apparently they've got a lead to follow up today.'

178

Valentine stood up, stepped away from his desk. 'So on top of everything we're two men down today.'

'It could be worse,' said McCormack.

'How, just how could it be worse, Sylvia?'

'We could be three men down.'

'Just hold that very thought.' Valentine headed for the door.

32

As he stood in front of the vending machine waiting for his coffee cup to fill, Valentine told himself that he'd had a long career, and it wasn't without merit. There had been the predictable lows too, and the encounter with CS Martin that awaited him was definitely going to be another of those, but he had a lot to be proud of.

When he'd taken a knife in the heart, and been declared dead, that would have been a good enough reason for many to leave the force but he stayed on. He knew that financially, he really had no option though. And now that they'd moved to a bigger house, and moved his father in with them, those restraints had only tightened. The girls' demands were growing more costly every year and there'd be university to consider soon. Clare's spending might have been curtailed for now but that was a result of their huge splurge of late, she would be back to her old ways as soon as the sheen of a new house wore thin. A dull ache started deep inside his chest, somewhere in his damaged heart.

The DI picked up the cup, watched the slow trail of steam rising; the sharp aroma signalled the coming bitter assault on his tastebuds. He wouldn't miss the King Street coffee, that was for certain. He turned towards the long corridor and made his way to the chief super's office. He took a sip, it was hot, burning, and he jerked the cup away too quickly: a sliver of grey liquid landed on his white shirt front.

'Shit.' She'd notice that, right away. Dino was always pointing out the minor flaws that everyone else ignored, she presented them like evidence she was gathering to back up her own superiority.

Valentine rubbed at the coffee stain with his cuff, spreading the mark to a wider surface and transplanting some of it to the pristine cuff.

'What's the point?'

He knocked on the door and stepped back.

Silence. Maybe she'd gone out. He wished.

'Come . . .' Why did she always say that? It was like some ridiculous parody of a company boss from a seventies sit-com. As he opened the door he found he was grinning to himself.

'Should I deduct from your demeanour that you've had a break, Bob?' said Martin.

'I always caution the team against wild deductions, chief.' It was a bad start, and he knew it.

'Sit down, Bob.'

She closed the desk diary she'd been studying, sat back and pointed her elbows to the floor. There was a pause that lasted for a few seconds and then she snatched a deep breath and started to speak. 'It's hard to know where to begin with you.'

Valentine stayed calm, ignored the fact that he already felt like a child visiting the headmaster.

'I mean, it's as if you're trying to provoke me with all

these nonsensical actions.' She paused again, seemed to be waiting for the DI's response, when she saw that none was on the way she raised her voice. 'Do you know who my first call was from this morning?'

'I don't.'

'William Reynolds, I'm sure the name doesn't ring a bell, but when I tell you he's the boss of a Dr Caruthers that you've been upsetting at Ayr Hospital then you might get the gist.'

'Oh, right.'

'Yes, Bob. Reynolds is chief executive of the local health board, not someone we want to fall out with given how often we're in and out of their facilities.'

Valentine played with the crease in his trousers. 'Look, does this Reynolds bloke know that Sandra Millar is a murder suspect?'

'I don't care if he does or not, Bob. I don't want you upsetting him, or Dr Caruthers, or Major Rutherford, or the tea lady in the canteen at Killie Hospital, these are people we have to work with, our community, remember that.'

When she'd stopped shouting her voice reverberated in Valentine's ears. 'Do you understand me, Bob?'

'Yes, I understand.' He pushed away the crease in his trousers, brushed at his thighs as he tried to provide a defence. 'It's not been the easiest of cases . . .'

'Now, I'll stop you right there. None of the cases you handle are easy, Bob. You're a murder squad detective, that in itself should give you a clue as to what to expect in your in-box.'

'I'm well aware what it is I do. If I can be allowed to finish . . .' He glanced at the chief super, she tightened her mouth. 'This case, chief, is not your classic hot-blooded murder. It might look that way, but every time we take a step forward we're yanked three steps back. It's not straightforward, not a matter of joining all the dots in the constellated disadvantage, there's more to this, much more.'

'Bob, I've had two hospitals complain about you since Tulloch was stabbed, I've had to hose down the bloody army because of your attitude and to top it all, no, to put the cherry on the top of this steaming pile of shit that you are calling a murder investigation – and I've been through your files so I know what I'm talking about – I find out you've been withholding evidence from me.'

Valentine uncrossed his legs, as he leaned towards Dino's desk, the temptation to scream back at her was only halted by his ramping heart rate and the warnings of his medics about stress. He eased himself back in his chair and drew breath.

'The post-mortem report was an oversight on my part.'

'What was that?'

'I'd like to apologise, there's no excuse for not passing that on immediately. I should have done, and I didn't.'

The admission blindsided the chief super. She clearly didn't believe she was hearing it. 'Are you trying to cover for someone on the squad – Ally forget to deliver it to me, did he?'

'No. It was my fault.'

'Well it wasn't Phil, he's too bloody anal about admin. Was it that Glasgow girl, Sylvia?'

'I just told you. I take full responsibility, it was an oversight.'

'And you're not even going to play the old overloaded-with-work tune?'

The DI stalled, he hadn't expected her to react in this manner. He'd made a serious error, she had every right to question his judgement, suspend him or worse. But now it seemed like she suspected him of reverse psychology, a double bluff that she refused to fall for, only the truth was much simpler.

They stared at each other over the desk, dredging each other's gaze for a solution to the impasse. The silence was broken by the telephone sounding like a bell between rounds.

'Hello, CS Martin.'

It felt like an intrusion to listen to the call, Valentine got up and paced around the room. The conversational tone of the call had quickly changed, concern crept into the chief super's voice. She crouched over her desk now, slouched into the receiver like it was her only means of support.

'What . . . Say that again . . . When?'

CS Martin didn't move, her shoulders appeared locked in a downward-facing angle to the desk, where her free hand was a tense fist.

Valentine became aware of the rapid change in the room's atmosphere. He returned to his seat and tried to look innocent whilst discerning what the talk was about.

'Wait, are you telling me this is related?' she said.

'Shall I go?' said Valentine.

She flagged him down. 'And when did this call come in?

Have you spoken to the parents? Have they spoken to the press?'

He wanted to know what had happened.

'Right. Keep it that way. I'll meet you there right away.' The receiver was returned to its cradle.

'Sounds serious,' said Valentine.

'Your get-out-of-jail-free card.'

'I don't follow you.'

She stuck her jaw towards him. 'Well, I'm not talking about the divi commander's team-building exercise, though God alone knows what I will tell him about that . . . Look, if you ever conceal evidence from me again, Bob, or even think about bullshitting me, I'll have your arse in a sling.'

'Point taken. Can I ask about the call?'

'We have another one.' She eased herself away from behind the desk, stood up and walked towards the coat stand in the corner of the room.

'Another murder?' It didn't seem possible, the case was beyond complex already.

'That's right. And it's yours.'

'So it's related to the Tulloch murder?'

'Clever lad.' She started to fasten the buttons of her navy-blue fitted coat. 'At least that's the assumption I'm making right now given we have a body matching the description of a missing person that was reported last night by the parents of Jade Millar's boyfriend.'

Valentine followed as the chief super made for the door. 'Niall Paton was reported missing?'

'That's right. Parents rocked in last night and spilled their hearts to Jim on the front desk. We also had some calls on unusual activity out at the old pits, sounded like fly-tipping but Jim put two and two together and we've had uniform out since first light.'

'Why didn't someone inform me?'

'Oh I was informed, Bob.' She grinned at him, but it was really for herself. 'It's a right pain in the arse when your colleagues keep stuff from you, isn't it?' She stepped through the door, left it swinging open for Valentine to follow.

'Two wrongs don't make a right,' he yelled.

'No, Bob, they don't.' She stopped at the top of the stairs, turned. 'And don't think I'd be so petty, as you're very fond of saying this is a murder investigation and one I was about to remove from you until it became a double murder investigation. Count yourself lucky you're still on the job and don't expect to get any more leeway from me now.'

33

DI Bob Valentine's arrival in Cumnock was like any other visit to his former hometown: uneasy. There had been a time when coming home was a welcome event, he'd visit his parents and visit his past, but those days were gone. There was nothing for him in Cumnock now. If he was being honest, and dispassionate, he would have said there was nothing in Cumnock at all now. There had been work, once. Mines with a hundred years of coal that Thatcher shut up and flooded lest anyone try to reverse her decision. His father had mined those pits.

There were the streets lined with black spit, the talk of the Friday-night pint that generally ended on a Sunday, and throughout it all, the hard-worn Cumnock women who always kept a clean front step scrubbed twice a day. The town had changed now, and the changeover had been brief. The town had gone from his home to a place not fit for animals in a few short years. The idea that dole moles and junkies might ever care about their front step amused him now.

'Something funny?' said the chief super.

'The old toon . . .'

'You grew up here didn't you, father a miner?'

'Yes, on both counts.' They stood on the edge of the field where uniformed officers were busying themselves with blue and white tape, not quite sure whether it was appropriate to tie-up bramble bushes. 'Place is a mystery to me now, though.'

'It's bloody Cumnock, the place is a mystery to everyone. Need your head tested to stay here now.'

'Or have no choice.' Valentine turned to face CS Martin, 'That's the thing though, we had no choice when I was growing up, but people cared then. People made the most of the place.'

A tut. 'I can't see this lot bothering their backside. We're too far gone now, Bob. Places like this were written off years ago. You're well and truly out of it . . . Come on, our stiff awaits.'

Valentine watched and waited as the chief super negotiated a dry-stone dyke. She made noisy objections each time the stones wobbled under her hands and her coat tails rode up in comical fashion as she descended the dyke. She was still cursing when she reached the field, the grass brushing the hem of her coat and forming a wet tide line. It was a bizarre scene for the detective, so out of place, so strange to see his boss wading through a field by the town where he'd once watched his father set off for the pit with a lunch pail under his arm. He felt like he had lived two lives, that they should never have crossed, but here he was watching his present attaching to his past. If there was a message to be discerned, it escaped him; but the eerie feeling that he should be drawing some kind of meaning from the event turned inside him.

'We should have brought wellies,' CS Martin roared over the wet grass.

'Wait till you get further in, you'll be calling for waders.'

'That better be a joke.'

'No joke. You'll need bloody scuba gear if you fall down one of the shafts.'

The chief super halted her stride, turned to one of the uniformed bodies. 'How far do we have to go?'

'Just a little bit further.' The uniform pointed. 'Over there, where the tracks end.'

Valentine caught up with them. 'Tell me they're our tracks and we're not parading half the force through our crime scene.'

The uniform shrugged, looked blankly ahead. It seemed too complicated a question for him to understand, never mind answer.

'Christ, I knew it. We're up to our knees in it, stamping all over potential evidence.'

'Relax, Bob. I'm sure if there's any footprints in this muck we've already got them cast.'

The DI peered up to the sky, but didn't offer a reply; he'd trust his insights into the way uniform worked over the chief super's any day of the week. As he looked at the churned mess of the ground he knew if there had been anything of use there it was now gone. The fresh path cut through two fringes of flattened long grass that stretched all the way from the drystone dyke. Up ahead the SOCOs in white suits were shuffling about, the unearthly starkness of their appearance always made Valentine aware of the close proximity of death. The dream, or whatever it was, where he had met Bert returned to him. The message had been to look for a soldier but he knew that wasn't what he was going to find here.

As they reached the main area of activity, Valentine was handed a box of rubber gloves, he took a pair and passed them to CS Martin.

'No thanks,' she said. 'I'm prepared to observe but I draw the line at poking about in fusty remains.'

'Whatever you say.' Valentine snapped a glove onto his wrist. 'You might want the blue slippers, though, keep your shoes clean.'

'Is that supposed to be a sexist remark?'

'If it is I'm not aware of it.'

'Women and shoes, y'know . . .'

Valentine knew all about women and shoes, his wife had a theory that it was something she fixated on herself because it was the only part of her body that hadn't grown. The DI eyed Martin but kept the observation to himself and approached the depute fiscal.

'Hello, Col,' he said.

'Ah, detective. Hello to you too.'

The prat knew it was detective inspector and Valentine knew that he knew it but let it slide. Colin Scott fed on irritating people, the worst move was always to show they'd got to you. 'I take it you're done here?'

'All yours, you can . . . *do as thou wilt.*'

'That . . . *shall be the whole of the law.*' Valentine's retort put the fiscal on guard, police – even detective inspectors – weren't supposed to be educated enough to finish his obscure quotations.

'Christ, get a room you pair.' Martin marched between them, approached the huddle of SOCOs.

It was a patchy piece of ground, bare mostly. The grass halted about four feet away and a muddy expanse, like a dam, had pooled brown water on one side. There was clearly a source for the water somewhere but Valentine couldn't spot it. As he moved closer to the group of uniforms and SOCOs he surmised that a flooded pit was the cause; and then he caught a glimpse of a grey-white face that was no longer human.

The young man had deep hollows where his eyes should be and a gape of mouth that had been shaped into an unnatural droop. Valentine saw the jaw was broken, it was too wide to be a natural opening. The victim lay on his back, a bony chest exposed to the elements showed bruising, deep-coloured contusions and lighter, yellowing finger marks. He'd been beaten. Blood pooled beneath the nose, around the eyes and to the sides of the black gaping mouth. He was young, that was clear, but not the youngest corpse the detective had seen.

'Just a boy, isn't he?' said Valentine.

'Just a lad of sixteen summers,' said Martin.

'We've provisionally ID'd him then?'

'Yes.' She pushed past the DI, moved closer to the pale body. 'I should have said, shouldn't I? Must be annoying that, being kept in the dark.'

He didn't respond, it seemed to be a day for holding back.

'It's Niall Paton, the details match our description from the parents.' Martin crouched down. 'He'll need a good clean-up before we do a formal ID. He's been battered black and blue, obviously pissed somebody off.'

He squatted down beside the chief super. 'Or had something somebody wanted.'

'He's sixteen, though, what could he have had that anyone wanted, an Xbox?'

'Information, maybe. Like the whereabouts of Jade Millar, or her brother, or her brother's old army buddy.'

Martin got up, she was still looking over the body as she spoke. 'Careful, Bob, you'll be making it sound like somebody on your squad knocked him off.'

It was a low blow. 'We're keen to find them all, but so are one or two others.'

'Like who?'

Valentine rose. 'Well I had an interesting chat with Eddy Harris recently, it appears one of the Meat Hangers staff has gone missing since the robbery. I'd think Norrie Leask would be very keen to find him.'

'Well why don't you ask him?'

'I would, but Leask's gone missing too.'

The chief super removed a packet of Regal from her coat pocket and lit up. 'Who is this that works for Leask?'

'A bloke called Finnie, used to be in the army with Darry Millar and, it turns out, Tulloch.'

'They were all in Tom Rutherford's regiment?'

'That's right. Makes you wonder what Major Tom's hiding, does it not?'

She drew deeply on the cigarette, exhaled a long stream of smoke. 'That's all I bloody need, a military police investigation on my patch.'

192

'None of the victims are military, I think that rules them out.'

'Oh, not necessarily, Bob. If there's a military angle they have the strangest way of making it their business. And that could leave us with two unsolved murders on our books, or worse, two collars taken off our crime stats, which we can ill afford.'

Valentine let the chief super talk herself out, she was extracting a final gasp from her cigarette when he spoke again. 'Have the boy's parents been informed?'

'Oh, shit. No, they only told us he was missing last night.'

'It's going to be a bloody shock for them, after they've only reported him missing. Do you want me to let them know?'

'Yes, Bob, you do that.' She held up the cigarette, got ready to flick it onto the ground; Valentine reached over and snatched the filter tip from her fingers.

'I'll put that out.'

'Great. Cheers. You want to drive back too?'

The DI nodded. 'Why not?'

In the car CS Martin spoke in a near-whisper. 'You don't think the robbery and the murders are connected do you?'

'I think the robbery and the murders and the army are all connected in some way, my only problem is that I've got no idea how.'

'This is a mess.' She grabbed a handful of hair and leaned on the window. 'I don't want you to antagonise the military. If you have to ask questions, do it on the quiet, or do it through my office.'

'And what about the Meat Hangers?'

'Tie in with DI Harris, if there's a likely connection, you can take his team into your squad. The way things are shaping up, you're going to need the extra numbers.'

34

The temperature outside was warming, the sun high and visible for the first time in ages. Some of the school kids from the academy were already larking about in the heat, playing slapsie and chasing each other. It made the detective think of Niall Paton – he couldn't have been much older than many of the kids, going on the picture his parents had shown him an hour earlier.

The Patons were clueless as to their son's disappearance and desolate at the news of his murder. Valentine had watched the mother fall into her husband's arms and weep, repeating the word 'why' over and over. He had no answer for that, and he knew he had no answer for many more questions that were stacking up around him.

The family lived in a nice house, only a few streets from where he used to live in Masonhill. That their son had hooked up with Jade Millar – a girl from Whitletts – made him curious. They had such different backgrounds, one family was stable, the other a disaster. Had they really just hit it off? What was the attraction? The detective smiled to himself, he was being naive and he knew it.

He was biting into the sausage roll when he spotted DS McCormack approaching from the other side of the road.

He raised a plastic coffee cup to get her attention, waved her across.

'Some weather, this?' she said.

'Don't knock it, if the sunshine lasts another hour that's going to pass for our summer.'

She looked down the street. 'That you parked there?'

Valentine nodded. 'Yeah, come on. You can fill me in on your Meat Hangers visit as we go.' They turned to negotiate the pavement and were halted by a young mum with a pushchair, a noisy toddler covered in ice cream wailed at them. 'That looks good, son.'

The mother smiled, pride beaming out of her.

As they walked on, McCormack spoke. 'It was an interesting visit, but what John Greig might have called a game of two halves.'

'I'll have the good half first . . .'

'Well, I got in, I suppose that's a positive given that the place is closed up. Had to rattle Leask's accountant for the key and a tour of the records but he played along. No idea where Leask is, though.'

'What's Eddy Harris saying about that?'

'He's been on the knocker but drawing blank stares all over. If anyone does know where Leask is, they're not saying.'

'Jesus, he can't just disappear, he's not Houdini, this is a low-rent scrote we're talking about here. I wouldn't have rated Leask with the marbles. And what about his business, are you telling me he's just put the shutters on it?'

McCormack brightened. 'Ah, now that's where things get interesting. Bullough, the accountant, says the takings had been down for a long time, Leask was looking to wind up the business. The robbery would have been the final nail in the coffin he reckons because Leask had cash-flow problems.'

'And he just gave this information up freely, did he?'

A half-smile. 'Not exactly. Though once he knew we were talking about a double murder, and that we might need to take him in for questioning, the hankie came out to dab his brow.'

'OK.' Valentine scrunched up the remainder of his sausage roll and binned it. 'Go back to the robbery, do you know what the tally was on the take?'

'A whole bunch. Can't say for sure because the books haven't been done for that weekend but it's a Friday night and Saturday night's takings which get kept in the safe because there's no bank on those days, then you add in the Sunday night's too, which couldn't be banked until the Monday, only nobody works a Monday because they're in all weekend. . .'

Valentine held up a hand. 'Right, stop there. It's three night's takings, is that what you're telling me?'

'And the Saturday alone usually totals ninety grand.'

'We're talking a six-figure sum, which is not to be sniffed at.'

'The insurance payout would dig Leask out of a big hole, let's put it that way.'

They'd reached the car, Valentine pointed the key at the door. 'Hang on, if Leask was doing an insurance job, then why the vanishing act? Surely he'd just hide the loot and wait for the Man from the Pru showing up with a cheque. It doesn't make any sense, as it stands.'

McCormack opened the car door. 'That's exactly what I thought.'

'So it only makes sense if Leask's plan has gone awry, if someone's done a number on him.'

'Do you think that's what happened to James Tulloch?'

Valentine got in the car, sat behind the wheel. They were both staring into the packed street as he spoke. 'I have honestly no idea, Sylvia. I wouldn't even like to speculate.'

'I hear you. The options are limitless aren't they?'

'They're up there.' Valentine turned the key in the ignition, flicked on the blinkers. 'We'll have to start narrowing them down. How did you get on with shaking up the staff at the Meat Hangers?'

'I didn't. There was no one there, it's padlocked up, remember? What I did get, though, was the full staff list, and Bullough confirmed that it's up to date.'

'He could be very useful to us, make sure he's kept on pins.'

'Oh, I have. Gave him the don't-leave-town-without-letting-us-know speech.'

'Right. Let's get back to the station and run those through the national computer. If there's a name on there with a record we might be lucky.'

'We haven't been so far.'

'Well that has to change some time, Sylvia.'

35

Darry Millar sought out the bar by following a faded tartan carpet that was held together by spillage stains. The yellowing woodchip on the walls was scuffed and scarred but looked fresh compared to the original dado rail, a sallow shade of yellow that might once have been magnolia. Above the door it had said guest house but he knew it wasn't an accurate description: they wouldn't get away with doss house, though. At the bar – which smelled of damp raincoats and cheap whisky – he removed a ten-pound note from the pocket of his jeans and placed it on a sodden bar-towel.

'What can I get you?' The barman stooped as he spoke.

'A pint, please.'

'Heavy?'

'Yeah, that'll do.'

There was a television playing in the corner of the room, it was the news but he'd missed the headlines, they were onto the sports preview now. The barman stared, half-hypnotised, at the screen but managed to turn off the tap as the pint glass filled.

'Anything else?'

'Erm, yeah, any food on the go?'

A huff. 'We do lunches, but the kitchen's shut now.'

'What about a sandwich or something?'

'There's a garage up the road might have something. I can do crisps.'

Darry handed over his money and asked for two bags of crisps. It wasn't much but he'd have to take something back to Jade. As the barman returned Darry was sipping his pint, the taste soured as he caught sight of a familiar face on the television screen.

'Turn that up!'

The barman pointed a remote control at the corner of the room. The speakers crackled as the volume increased.

'*The body of a young Ayrshire man was found in a shallow grave near Cumnock today . . .*'

'Jesus Christ,' said Darry.

'You know this lad?'

He looked at the barman. 'No. No I don't. Just seems awful though. I mean, not a nice way to go.'

'There's no nice ways, son.'

He raised his pint, changed tack. 'There's the drink.'

As the barman walked away, returned to his seat at the other side of the till, Darry listened to the rest of the broadcast.

'*Niall Paton, a pupil of Belmont Academy in Ayr, was sixteen years old. Police say they are treating the death as suspicious and following a definite line of inquiry.*'

Darry couldn't finish his pint, he took the crisps and returned to the room where Jade was waiting. As he opened the door she had her mobile phone to her ear but switched it off immediately.

'Who was that?'

'Nobody. I mean, I was just checking my credit.' She put the phone in her pocket. 'Did you get anything to eat?'

Darry put the crisps on the bed. 'Look, I think you should sit down.'

'What?'

'Sit down, Jade. I've got something to tell you.'

She was rustling the crisp bags, opening them up and stuffing the contents in her mouth. 'Well, what is it?'

Darry went to sit beside her on the bed. His throat grew stiff, the words too difficult to form in his mouth. He sat silently, staring at the hands in his lap.

'I thought you had something to say,' said Jade.

'They killed Niall.' He blurted the words.

'What did you say?'

'The news, it was just on downstairs. They found Niall in Cumnock, he'd been murdered.'

Jade dropped the crisps on the bed, for a moment she looked to have misheard, but the reaction was merely delayed. She spun around and fell on the pillows, sobbing.

'I'm sorry, Jade.'

'You didn't even know him.'

'I didn't have to. It's tragic. He was just a boy.'

Jade turned around. 'He had nothing to do with any of this.'

'I know.'

'How can you feel sorry for him? *How*?' Darry leant over to reassure his sister, she pushed his comforting hand away. 'You didn't even know him. You'd only just met him.'

'I know, Jade, but he was looking after you, he was going to stand by you whatever.'

'He wasn't the father.'

'What did you say?'

She sat up on the bed, wiped her eyes with the sleeve of her cardigan. 'He was an idiot.'

'Don't say that, Jade. He was doing the right thing by you.'

'He was a bloody idiot. And I was just using him, we only had sex after I found out I was pregnant.'

Darry's imagination lit up, he didn't want to consider the options if Niall wasn't the father. 'Jade, stop it.'

'No. He should never have got involved with me, this is what happens to everyone who gets involved with me. Whether they like it or not they end up dead or their lives ruined, even Dad, even *you* soon if you're not careful.'

Darry turned to face his sister, grabbed her by the shoulders and started to shake her. 'Shut up, now. Do you hear me? I want you to stop that talk, it's nonsense and you need to think about more than yourself now.'

Jade dropped her head and fell into Darry's arms. 'I can't go on like this much longer.'

'You won't have to.'

'We can't keep running and hiding, we're going to run out of money soon. I can't keep this baby, I can't!'

'As soon as I get hold of Fin we'll get things sorted. If he'd just answer his bloody phone.'

'Fin can't sort anything. He can't get Mum away from the police.'

Darry pulled his hands away, tapped his temple. 'Mum's

202

not herself, that's why she's in hospital, Jade. Whether the police were there or not, we couldn't just take her away. She needs help, she's ill.'

Jade started to cry again. 'That's my fault too. It's all my fault.'

'No, it's not. I told you, I don't want you to think like that.'

'No. I mean it. You need to rest, get some sleep.'

Jade curled into a ball on the bed and Darry helped her off with her jacket. She cried and shook where she lay and in a few moments she was sleeping, exhausted, but the torments of earlier a long distance away.

Darry sat and stared at his sister on the bed: what was he going to do? There were no easy answers. Tulloch was dead, that was all that mattered. He was worried about his mother, but she would be better in the long run. She had seen Tulloch for what he was, and now she was free of him. Even if the police wanted to blame her, even if she was to blame, there was no way she could really be held responsible in her state of mind. It was all so messed up, there were no answers anymore. All he knew was that he had to get Jade away, and fast. He needed to find somewhere where they could work out what their next move was going to be because if the police found them now they would be split up and she'd be on her own. She had no one else. He couldn't let her down too.

As Darry reclined in the armchair, covered himself with Jade's coat, he felt her phone sitting in the inside pocket. He took it out, stared at the screen. He'd seen her talking to someone when he came in and he wanted to know who it was. He called up the last number, it was a mobile, but he didn't recognise the number.

Darry pressed dial.

The line started to ring.

'Hello, Jade . . . what happened?'

He knew the voice at once. '. . . *Finnie*.'

36

The incident room was buzzing when Valentine and McCormack returned. Most of the team were drinking coffee from tall Costa cups; by the number of discarded plastic containers littering the desktops it looked like a sandwich run had also been completed recently. The detectives moved towards the incident board and Valentine checked for any updates. The photographs of Niall Paton had been added, the extant one and the more recent images from the crime scene.

'Looks like a good working over,' said McCormack.

'No doubt about that. I wouldn't mind a look at Norrie Leask's knuckles right now.'

'I wouldn't think he'd get his own hands dirty with that sort of thing, sir.'

'No, you're right. He gets others to do the legwork. Get onto those staff records from the Meat Hangers, if you find anything give me a holler. I've got a debriefing with the Chuckle Brothers.'

'Are Ally and Phil back then?'

'Looks like it.' He pointed to the officers who stationed themselves in the glassed-off office at the other end of the incident room.

'Jeez, they look pensive.'

'Yeah, and not in a good way.'

McCormack headed to her workstation and Valentine made for the office, grabbing a coffee from the nearby tray as he went. A few heads rose from desks as he passed but they slunk back rapidly; no one had anything to say, nothing to add to the ongoing investigation. Valentine's stomach tensed with the prospect of what his team were facing.

It had been a tough time, visiting the Patons and telling them he thought the son they had reported missing was lying in the morgue. Asking them to identify the boy, as he lay there bruised and battered, had been even more painful. There was never a nice time to tell anyone that a loved one had been taken from them, but a child murder was a brutal undertaking. For Valentine, this was the second killing on his patch lately, and he didn't want to see another one.

As he opened the door to the office Donnelly and McAlister acknowledged the DI with downtrodden nods.

'Christ, I hope the hangdog looks aren't an indicator that your jolly to the east was a complete waste,' said Valentine.

McAlister looked to Donnelly, his heavy eyes pleaded for a reply. They were worn out, tired. 'It depends what you want to hear, boss,' said Donnelly.

'I'll settle for our perp in the cells and Dino slobbering over a bone with a big bow on it. Of course, the way things are going, I have a feeling you're going to tell me the case is being taken over by the boys with MP on their arms.'

'I'm not entirely sure what we've got,' said McAlister, scratching a stubbled chin.

Valentine moved behind his desk, pulled the chair under him. 'You'll have heard about the Paton boy.'

'Yes. No age at all was he.'

'He was sixteen, Phil. And no, that's no bloody age at all.' Valentine told the detectives about the recent links that had been discovered to the Meat Hangers robbery before skirting over the run-in he'd had with the chief super.

'She's a paranoiac, thinks we're all talking about her,' said McAlister.

'We are,' said Donnelly, a rare smile creeping in.

'But, what I'm saying is, we should never have kept the pathology report from her, was just asking for trouble.'

'Well, that was my call,' said Valentine. 'So, I'll take the fall for that one. But I had my reasons . . . Now from here on, we keep Dino in the loop, we won't get away with it again.'

'Not a chance.'

'None. And unless you fancy answering to Flash Harris you'll take heed . . . Now, tell me about your visit to the barracks.'

The pair exchanged glances once more and McAlister conceded to Donnelly's claim on the initial briefing.

'It was a tough gig, as you might imagine,' said Donnelly.

'I didn't expect them to lay out the red carpet.'

'No. They didn't, nothing like it in fact. But we persisted. The first day was gathering names, people who knew Tulloch and Millar.'

Valentine cut in. 'What about Grant Finnie?'

'We just heard about him, funnily enough, about the same time you did by the looks of things.'

'Go on . . .'

'Well, you know that Tulloch was about as popular as a turd in a jacuzzi, but he was a higher rank too, a sergeant to be precise and he had a bit of a rep as a ball-buster. Millar and Finnie were both under his command but when we put that to some of the squaddies they clammed up, it was very strange, almost rehearsed.'

'What do you mean by that?'

'Like they were all reading from the same script, like they'd been told to keep schtum.'

'By who?'

'No idea, boss,' said Donnelly. 'Higher up the ladder I'd expect but that could be anyone. Of course, it could be the institutionalised mind-set – no one in the army wants to be seen as a grass.'

Valentine touched his brow. 'Hang on, you've just told me no one was saying anything.'

McAlister spoke: 'Officially, that's true. Unofficially, and I mean off the record, we got a hint that something had went on between Tulloch and Finnie.'

'Like what?'

'It was in Helmand, on a tour of duty in late 2013.'

Valentine found himself dipping his head towards the desk, there was a sound, a voice he recognised that shouldn't be in the room. He heard Bert's words again and began to feel queasily unwell.

McAlister got up and prodded Valentine's shoulder. 'You OK there, boss?'

The room's mood returned to normal, the DI snapped, 'I'm fine. What happened in Helmand?'

Donnelly joined McAlister standing in front of Valentine's desk. 'We don't know. But we can guess that it wasn't pleasant.'

'Try highly irregular,' said McAlister. 'We spoke to one of the boys from the regiment off the base, that's why we needed to stay a bit longer. He told us that there was an incident, a crime of some sort and he thought it involved one of the women on the ground, a native . . .'

'What happened?'

'We don't know for sure.'

'Well, are we talking rape or torture?'

'Boss, we're talking murder.'

'She was killed?'

'Shot,' said Donnelly, his voice a low drawl.

'That's a bloody war crime, no wonder they hushed it up, can you imagine the fallout in the media?' Valentine got to his feet. 'How much of this have you confirmed?'

'On the record?'

'Don't piss about, Ally, on the record, off the record, we're not in the business of protecting murderers.'

Donnelly held up his palms. 'Look, our informant stuck his neck out.'

'What about that bloody woman, Phil? What about Tulloch and Niall Paton? They stuck their necks out too. I need more to go on than a rumour.'

'We checked the books, I mean the official paperwork. It all ties up, the times. Tulloch and Finnie were in Helmand together at the same time, returned together at the same time, but their departure wasn't at the same time as the regiment shipped out.'

'That's hardly conclusive.'

'No, but their discharge papers might be. They were booted out the Royal Highland Fusiliers on the same day, and they both hit civvie street without so much as a kind word from the army about their spud-peeling skills.'

37

The incident room was a blur of unfamiliar faces, bodies that were no more than obstacles and a low-level hum that might have been chatter but might also have been the inside of Valentine's head cracking. He wasn't in an unfamiliar place, the opposite was true, but it was certainly an uncomfortable place. His booming senses and eddying emotions told him that the return had been instant, round about the time Phil had detailed the results of the east-coast investigation.

'Sir, can I have a word?' It was DS McCormack.

'Not now, Sylvia.'

'It's important.'

'I'm sure it is, but it'll have to wait.' Valentine headed for the door and crossed the corridor in loping strides. He tried to increase his pace but the effort didn't bring the desired results, only made him feel more off balance. He reached out for the wall to steady himself and almost fell against it. He stopped, gathered breath and made the final steps to the door of the gents in an almost drunken stupor.

Inside, the door closed, the atmosphere changed. The sounds changed, the clatter of the incident room was replaced by a still almost hypnotic birr from the strip lights. He heard a voice and at once knew it didn't belong to anyone that existed on the same plain as him. There might have been actual words, and meaning attached to those, but the DI was too unsettled to allow himself to strain for their meaning. He rushed to the sink and started to splash cold water on his face and neck.

The water was a comfort, eased his rising temperature but failed to shake him from the moment. As Valentine straightened himself before the mirror his vision blurred then receded into darkness. As his sight returned he was holding tight to the skin, staring into the mirror at an image of a face he knew wasn't his. Somewhat higher than his right shoulder stood Bert McCrindle, fully suited in khaki, a cap perched at an angle above one eye.

'It's not right, son,' he said.

'What?'

Bert turned to the side, peered through Valentine. As the detective followed his gaze he saw another figure had joined them. At his left shoulder, in the mirror, was a young girl, she had black hair pulled tightly from her face. Although dark-skinned she looked pale, far too pale.

Bert spoke again. 'It's not right, son. They buried that girl in a shallow grave.'

'Who is she?'

As he stared at the girl in the mirror she turned to face Bert. She smiled, almost a bow, but Valentine's gaze was drawn to the small hole in her temple, a little black point the size of a fingertip that oozed a line of dark blood.

'Not right to treat another human life like that, son,' said Bert.

The detective took his gaze from the girl and returned to

Bert, as he did so, his blood surged and the strip lights burned hard and bright in his eyes. The intensity lasted only a few seconds before the blackness took over.

'Bob . . . Bob . . . Are you OK?' A new voice, familiar this time.

'Where am I?'

DS Donnelly came into focus, leaned down towards Valentine. 'You're in your office, here get this down you.'

'What is it?'

'Just water. You've had a tumble, Eddy there found you on the floor of the gents.'

DS McCormack started to press a cold can of Coke into his forehead. 'I don't think you've any injuries, there's no blood or bruising.'

'Lucky you never whacked your head off the sink,' said DS Harris. 'Luckier yet I found you when I did, you could have been there all day.'

Valentine pushed away the can of Coke. 'I'm grateful for your weak bladder, Eddy.' He waved away the assembled crowd. 'Look can you all get back to work, I've passed out, it happens, now get over it.'

'I think you should go home, take the rest of the day off, sir,' said McCormack.

'That'll be right. I'm fine, just been overdoing it lately, not had much sleep.'

Donnelly turned to McAlister and winked.

'I bloody saw that, Phil.'

'Sorry, boss. Just being funny.'

'Just being a dick you mean.'

'That's it, that's what I meant.'

Valentine pushed away his chair and stood up, he took a mouthful of water and followed it with two deep breaths. 'It's roasting in here . . .'

'I'll get the window open,' said McCormack.

'Wait, what was it you were going to say, when you stopped me on the way out earlier?'

'Oh, right, just that I ran the Meat Hangers staff through the database and we have a repeat offender, string of convictions for battery and a nice GBH cherry on top.'

Valentine put down the cup, reached over his desk to retrieve his jacket. 'Right, get moving. We're going to pay this one a visit . . . name?'

'Brogan, sir . . . Kyle Brogan and he stays in the same part of town as Tulloch did.'

'Another trip to the badlands. Hope you like the sound of banjos, Sylvia.'

DS Donnelly stepped forward. 'What about us, boss? Do you want us to get onto Major Tom?'

'You're kidding aren't you? He'd eat you alive. No, you leave that to me, I'll talk to the chief super when I get back. We need to approach this carefully, the military have a love affair with the Official Secrets Act and if we go in boots first then we'll likely come out that way too.'

'Shall I update the super?'

'No, leave her to me as well. I'll take care of that personally. I want to know how she's going to approach it but I also want to see her eyes when I confirm for her that she's been had by her new Major buddy.'

DS Donnelly started to fiddle with the collar of his shirt.

'But what if Dino comes in sniffing around, if I hold this back then surely that's putting us in her bad books again.'

'I'm never out of her bad books and the way this case is going there'll be a few more joining me before long. I want you and Ally to get onto the boffins and chase a full report on the Paton kid, what can they tell us about how he died and if there's any useful forensics on him, preferably not his own.' Valentine turned away from Donnelly and faced DI Harris. 'Eddy, welcome on board. I'm sorry it wasn't in more auspicious circumstances but now we do have you, I'll be putting you to use right away. I want you to get onto the school, Belmont, and get names of all Niall Paton and Jade Millar's main associates. I also want to talk to any teachers that they shared and get hold of any others that clocked unusual behaviour from the pair of them in recent weeks. Likewise sports clubs and whatever else kids go in for. Oh, and GPs, and anywhere else they were attending like therapists or what have you, talk to them. I want insights, draw up their profiles.'

'Christ, that's a tall order, anything else whilst I'm at it?' snapped Harris. 'I could shove a broom up my arse and sweep the stairs too, I suppose.'

'There will definitely be more, Eddy, I just haven't thought of it yet.'

38

In the car DS McCormack started her questioning the second the doors had closed. Her face, tight in the jaw, inferred anger but there were other emotions playing in her cracking voice. 'What the hell was that?' she said.

'I don't know.' Valentine's reply sounded meek. 'Trust me, Sylvia, if I did, I'd let you know chapter and verse.'

'Well something happened. I know that look. So don't pretend that it was just another bout of stress or over-tiredness from the job. And don't think about getting creative and playing the low blood sugar card, either!'

Valentine turned the key, started to feed the steering wheel through his dry palms. As they left the car park and turned onto King Street he was aware that he hadn't responded to McCormack yet. The tension between them was building steadily but he was lost for a response. She wasn't going to accept the stock reply and he didn't have the focus to summon a more thoughtful answer.

'Look, what do you want me to say? I can't get to grips with this any better than you, or anyone else for that matter.'

'Maybe we need to call Hugh Crosbie again, I mean, if things have escalated for you.' McCormack removed her mobile from the black leather bag on her lap. She was scrolling through numbers as Valentine spoke. 'No. I mean, not yet.' They'd reached the crossroads at the racecourse, the traffic lights – forever red – had the cars backed up through both lanes. The DI pulled on the handbrake, there didn't seem to be any chance that they were going anywhere for a little while. 'The picture, you know the one I mean . . .'

'The one that Hugh drew for you?'

'That's the one.' Valentine fiddled with the gear stick, tapped fingers on top. 'I stuck it on the fridge and my dad saw it.'

McCormack interrupted, 'He recognised the man in the picture?'

'That's right. An old uncle, apparently. Some sort of relative anyway.'

'He was in uniform. Did he die in the War?'

The tense feeling inside the car seemed to be easing, McCormack's tone dropping to a more rational level. 'No, actually, he didn't. I don't know him, I never did, but my dad said he came back from the war with shell shock, only it wasn't from the bombing. There was some kind of incident he was involved in, something that scared him for the rest of his days. He was a strange one, a loner, by all accounts for ever more. I think my mother knew the full story but she only touched on it with my father, it was the kind of thing that Dad wouldn't mention, personal y'know, like something he wouldn't want another man knowing, or even feel comfortable discussing.'

'Christ above, well you know what that sounds like to me: a sexual assault.'

'I thought so, too. There must have been plenty of that sort of thing going on in wartime. I think he endured it because of the era he lived in, men just didn't speak up about it, there was far too much shame involved.'

The traffic started to ease, the bumper ahead moved off. Valentine selected first gear.

'This all sounds very familiar,' said McCormack.

'War is hell, you mean?'

'No. It's familiar to the Tulloch and Finnie case in Afghanistan.'

'The second Phil and Ally came back with the story from the lad in the barracks. It was like I could feel, no *sense*, the connection.'

'The gents, this is what you're building up to? You passed out because something happened in there and I don't think it was a pissing contest with Flash Harris.'

Valentine broke into a weak smile. 'Everything's a pissing contest with Harris. But, yes, you're right. I saw something. But that wasn't the first time. There's been nightmares, sweats, visions . . . Just like on the Janie Cooper case. I know things are getting worse though because I saw Bert, just like that time in Glasgow when I saw Janie, do you remember when I passed out?'

'You wouldn't let me call an ambulance.'

'For all the good it would have done me, Sylvia. I'm strangely at ease with this today, it's like familiar territory now. I was scared witless when it happened to me the first time and the nightmares, they're horrific but not terrifying anymore. I don't know, I really don't know what I'm saying.'

'No. I understand. You're becoming inured to the visions, it's like Hugh Crosbie said, you learn to separate yourself from the actual situation and become an observer of it.'

'I wouldn't go that far, I mean, I wouldn't say I was comfortable enough in the situation to sit back and watch. It takes a toll, there's a physical side.'

'We should talk to Hugh again, I'm sure he'd be able to put you at ease that all of this is quite normal.'

Valentine spluttered, 'You're kidding aren't you? I'm a grown man, a professional law enforcer, I shouldn't be seeing ghosties.'

'Well, if you put it like that.'

'How else would I put it, Sylvia? I'm overwhelmed by this, it's playing with my head and my heart's not up to the strain. The only reason I'm not asking them to lock me up in the loony bin is because I sense that there's some meaning to all of this, that someone is trying to tell me something that will help solve these murders.'

'It worked before.'

'There's that too.' The DI turned into a side street and lowered his speed.

'The blackouts aren't good though, I worry about your health.'

'So do I, Sylvia. I wonder about the consequences, not for me but for Clare and the girls. Can you imagine the fallout for them if it got out? That's not my biggest concern right now though . . .'

'What's that then?'

'Back there, in the gents, I'm not sure what Harris saw.'

'Do you think he saw anything incriminating?'

'I don't know. I was out spark-cold. But if he did see something, I'm sure he won't be long in bringing it to my attention.'

'Or someone else's, that would be the real worry, Bob.'

'Yes, someone like Dino. She's putting up with me leading the investigation at the moment but I don't kid myself that it's because she thinks I'm the best man for the job. It would be all too easy for her to park me on psych leave for a while and then you'd all be dancing to Harris's tune.'

'Surely he wouldn't say anything, I mean, it's his word against yours.'

'And in that situation it comes down to who Dino has the most faith in. At the moment her faith in me is minimal.'

'Flash Harris doesn't have the best clear-up rate in the division, I can't see him holding any more sway with the chief super than you or anyone else. And there's the fact that this robbery is still unsolved . . .'

'There is that, but the robbery is our responsibility now, and once Harris familiarises himself with the two unsolved murders we have on our books then the robbery is going to play to his advantage with Dino – he'll have a running start. It's not looking good, Sylvia, any way you dice it.'

They'd reached the Whitletts home of Kyle Brogan. Valentine started to brake, in time to hear the street debris crunching under the car's tyres; stilled the engine and released his seatbelt.

McCormack retrieved her bag from the footwell and opened her door, said, 'So, what did this Bert guy tell you?'

Valentine walked around the vehicle, stopped when he faced her. 'The first time, something about finding the soldier. Today, in the gents, it wasn't so much what he said but what he showed me.'

'And what was that?'

The DI looked away, he was gripping the car keys in his fist as he stared into the middle distance. 'It was a sad-looking young girl, with a bullet in her head.'

39

DI Bob Valentine led the march up the path towards Kyle Brogan's home. The boxy council flats were surrounded by an assortment of broken children's toys, burst bin bags and rusting engine parts. A mattress from a single bed, that had been set on fire at some stage, was being used as a trampoline by a group of kids. One of the children, a boy in ripped trackies and a Rangers top, saluted the officers with a V-sign and sparked a spate of mimicry from the others.

'Little charmers,' said DS McCormack.

'You should acquaint yourself with them now, sure you'll be taking their details down the station in a few years.'

'Sooner for some of them, I'm sure.'

Outside the door Valentine tapped on a broken buzzer, the glass from the cover was lying smashed on the concrete doorstep; he pressed it with the sole of his shoe. 'You know what the problem here is, don't you?'

'Multiple deprived family units, constellated . . .'

Valentine cut her off. 'Stop that now! It's the state of this step. Look at it, my mother used to spend hours cleaning her front step. At around eleven o'clock every morning in the street I grew up in you could see women on their hands and knees scrubbing those steps, it was a point of real shame not to have a clean step.'

McCormack eased past the DI, pushed the door open. 'Fortunately, some of us have managed to get off our knees, sir. Which is a good job for the likes of you – might have been stuck outside this door all day without my help.'

'Fair play. I earned that.'

On the stairwell the detectives waded through discarded White Lightning bottles and cigarette ends. There was a strong smell of urine, a stronger smell of rotting refuse and a host of other smells that were largely unidentifiable but definitely not Chanel No. 5.

'Right, here we are, number 12b . . . give him a knock,' said Valentine.

Behind the door, with its chipped paint and exposed rot, came the sound of movement. Through the glass and the faded net curtain a dark shape of a slouching man was seen. He coughed, loudly, then cleared his throat. The next sound came from the letter box rattling, a hand was stuck through and a voice followed. 'What do you want?'

'Open up, Kyle, it's the rozzers,' said Valentine.

'I'm opening for no one, how do I know you're what you say you are? No, get lost.'

Valentine nodded towards McCormack, who removed her warrant card from her coat pocket and flashed it in front of the letter box. 'Please open the door, Mr Brogan.'

'Or it'll have a size-ten-shaped hole in it soon,' said Valentine.

A chain rattled, a key turned in the lock. As the rusty hinges cried out the door eased open. 'What's all this about?'

said Brogan. He was standing in chewing-gum-coloured vest and pants, eyes smarting at the flood of daylight he was forced to face.

'Can you not get some bloody clothes on, man?' said Valentine.

'I wasn't expecting visitors.' He put a hand over his eyes.

'Not this year, I see . . . When did you last change those Y-fronts?'

Brogan pointed a finger. 'That could be classed as harassment.'

McCormack replied, 'If I do it, will you call it sexual harassment?'

'I might.'

'Get inside, Mr Brogan. And don't make me laugh with your fantasies.'

The detectives proceeded through to the lounge, a small room at the front of the house where the curtains were closed. A brown sofa and a teak coffee table were the only concessions to furniture. Brogan, now dressed in tracksuit pants, removed a half-burnt cigarette from the edge of the table and lit it with a plastic lighter.

'What's this all about?' he said.

'Not working today, Brogan?' said Valentine.

'Shut down, isn't it? I'm a man of leisure, now.'

'That's very interesting, plenty of time to get into trouble.' He turned to McCormack. 'Show him the picture?'

She handed over a photograph of Niall Paton, the recent shot that his parents had supplied.

Brogan shrugged. 'I don't know him.'

'That's strange, your telly on the blink too?'

'No.' He indicated the television and flicked it on with the remote control.

'That photo you've got there is of a boy who was murdered the other night. We found him in a field in Cumnock, he'd been dumped down a shallow pit but the rain flushed him out. He wasn't a pretty sight.'

Brogan handed back the picture, he stood before them and folded his arms. 'What the bloody hell's that got to do with me?'

'Can you account for your movements over the last forty-eight hours, Mr Brogan?'

'I don't need to, Christ, I've done nothing wrong.' He drew heavily on the cigarette, it had gone out.

DS McCormack waved a hand at the sofa and invited Brogan to sit down again. 'Come on, Mr Brogan. This is a double murder investigation, we need you to be on your best behaviour.'

'Double murder. What? I mean, who else was done in?'

'Big Jim Tulloch,' said Valentine. 'Oh, you recognise the name, I see.'

'Only because I worked with him.'

'That would be at the Meat Hangers.'

'Aye, it was.'

'Norrie Leask's gone missing as well. Wonder if he'll turn up in a field in Cumnock next, Brogan?'

'I doubt it. Leask looks after himself, or has folk to do that.' He started to rub at his arms, lit another cigarette end that had been hiding behind his ear.

'Here, have one of mine,' said McCormack. She removed

a packet of Benson and Hedges and offered one to Brogan. He seemed to settle down once the cigarette was lit.

'OK,' said Valentine, 'I can see you're a little shaken up by all this unsettling news, never nice to hear a close friend's passed away.'

'Tulloch wasn't a friend of mine,' he spat the reply.

'Oh, I thought you were best mates, worked at the Meat Hangers together didn't you?'

'Aye, we worked together, that doesn't mean we were besties. Far bloody from it, mate. Big Tulloch was an arsehole, everyone will tell you that.'

'Everyone?' said McCormack. 'What about Grant Finnie?'

'Don't tell me Fin's dead as well . . .'

'No. Not that we're aware of. Friendlier with Finnie were you?'

'Friendlier than Tulloch, aye.'

Valentine moved towards the sofa, put his foot on the cushion next to Brogan. 'Now, if I was a right nosey bastard I'd be asking where all this animosity for our murder victim, James Tulloch, has come from. And then, I'd be asking why you're so friendly with a man who has gone missing, Grant Finnie, who may or may not be involved in Tulloch's demise.'

'Now wait a minute, I never said I was friendly with either of them.'

'Right now, Brogan, you're the only link I have between the two of them and the blagging at the Meat Hangers. Oh, and did I mention that Norrie Leask has gone missing and also a substantial amount of cash?'

Brogan drew heavily on the cigarette butt. 'I don't know anything about that.'

'Oh, no. I think you do. And what's more, I don't think I'm leaving here unless you tell me just exactly what you do know.' Valentine sat down beside him on the sofa.

'Now look, I'm not saying I know anything, all I can tell you is there was some kind of problem, I don't know what you'd call it, a feud maybe, between Big Jim Tulloch and Fin.'

'Go on.'

'Tulloch was always needling him, Fin that is. I think it went way back, I've no idea what it was about but Tulloch was the one with the problem. See, Fin was there first and Tulloch got his job later, it was like he only took the job to stick it to Fin, on a daily basis like.'

'And you say this went way back.'

'I don't know how far back, they were in the army together but you'll know that.'

'And how do you know the animosity went so far back, it could have just kicked off at the Meat Hangers, maybe Tulloch thought he should still have been Fin's boss?'

'No, it was an old wound. It was common knowledge after the punch-up.'

Valentine glanced at McCormack. 'What punch-up?' said the DI.

'They went to blows one night, round the back of the club, it was a fair go as well, crates and barrels were flying.' Brogan brightened at the memory. 'It was stopped right enough, by Leask's boy, that Joe fella with the gold chains and the leather jacket. Another big knuckle-dragger.'

'And when was the fight?' said McCormack.

'Not long ago, month or so maybe.'

'And there was no trouble after that?'

'Nah, not really. They kept them apart, surprised they never got their jotters, mind.'

'Why didn't Leask sack them?'

'You tell me, he's never usually shy about throwing folk out the door.' Brogan shot off the sofa, irritated. 'Right, is that enough for you? Can I get on with my life now?'

Valentine stood up to face him, motioned McCormack to the door. 'Don't go straying far, Brogan. I might want a word with you again.'

Outside the building, Valentine looked up to the flat they had just came from. Kyle Brogan was standing at the window, a yellowing net curtain pulled back. He made brief eye contact with the officers then removed his cigarette and nodded.

'What do you think?' said McCormack.

'He's a lying little scrote. That's what I think.'

'You think he made that up about the fight?'

'No. I don't think he's got the imagination for that. I think that was instinctual on his part, he just gave us something to get rid of us. There's more inside that manky little skull of his, though.'

The sound of the window opening drew the officers' gaze to Brogan, he was leaning onto the ledge now, said, 'And I hope you'll tell your wee pal what I told you as well . . . I'm playing nice like he said.'

Valentine nodded once to McCormack then sprung back to Brogan. 'You just stay right where you are, boyo!'

The officers started back for the door of the flats.

40

Darry Millar was the last person Fin expected to call on Jade's mobile phone. The messages from Leask had mounted to such a ridiculous level that he'd ditched his previous phone and taken a new number. It had been his intention to let Darry have the new number, eventually, but his first priority had been to Jade. The girl had always had more than her fair share of problems but the situation she now found herself in was as bad as it got. It shouldn't have happened, not after all he knew about Tulloch.

'Hello, Darry,' he said.

'You thought it was Jade.'

'I . . . I did yeah.'

There was a prolonged silence between them. 'Why's my sister got your new number and I haven't?'

'I was going to give you it, but it's been a bit crazy of late.'

'I've noticed, Fin. You might not think it but there's a lot I've noticed lately.' Darry's voice hid an accusation.

'What's that supposed to mean?'

He didn't answer the question. 'Jade's fine. She's here, with me.'

'That's good. I'm glad.'

'Are you?'

Fin's voice rose. 'Of course it's good. Jesus, if she wasn't with you she'd be in the same spot as your mum now.'

'You're talking about my mum now? She's in some state, I don't think she'll ever be making the finals of *Mastermind*, her brain's scrambled.'

The raised voice subsided. 'I hear she's in hospital, best place for her I suppose.'

'Better than where Niall is.'

'I suppose.'

The sound of a ferry's horn blared in the background. 'Fin, tell me what happened, I mean in your words.'

Fin looked out of the guest house window, the passenger boat was docking at Brodick pier. He tried to think what to say to his friend but couldn't locate the words. He paced the room, looked at the bed, the rucksack, the pile of money.

'Fin, what the hell happened?'

'Well, what did Jade say?' he sounded coy.

'She hasn't said much that makes any sense.'

'Well what makes you think I can add to that?'

'She said that Tulloch got what he deserved.'

Fin lowered himself onto the bed, the room was too warm and the over-complicated pattern on the wallpaper blurred. 'Did she tell you about . . .'

'What?'

'About the . . . Christ, I have no right telling anyone. Ask her, God Almighty, man, this has been hard enough for me, I don't need this from you too!'

Darry's voice came slow and calm. 'She told me she's pregnant, if that's what you mean?'

'It should never have happened.'

'No, it shouldn't, Fin. You were supposed to be minding her. I was still on tour, I couldn't get home even if I wanted to. I trusted you, you were my friend and what was it you said, *I'll look out for her, I'll keep an eye on her.*'

'Darry, if you only knew what I've been through for her, for you too.'

A laugh, deep and guttural. 'My heart bleeds for you, *mate.*'

'It wasn't meant to be like this.'

'Oh, no. I bet it wasn't. I misjudged you, I thought you would never let me down but it turns out I never knew you at all. I'm wondering now what I should read into those stories you told me about what Tulloch did in Helmand.'

Fin spat, 'Stories. You think I made that up?'

'How am I to know? Maybe the army knew something the rest of us didn't when they dumped you both.'

'I can't believe I'm hearing this. You were there when I spoke out, you saw the mess I was in. Bloody hell, Darry, they flung me out the army for reporting him, for speaking out against what he did. Do you really think I could make that up?'

'I don't know what's true and what's false anymore, Fin. All I know is my sister is up the pike, her young life ruined, and my mother is looking at the rest of her life in a padded cell because you brought that bastard to our home.'

Fin flared, 'He trailed me home, came looking for me, I never brought him. He was a psychopath, he wanted to make me pay. Jesus, he blamed me for ruining his career, his life.'

'Then why did he ruin mine?'

'I don't know. Because you were the closest I had to family, because he wanted to see me burn, because he could. Because he was nuts.' As he stopped screaming into the phone, Fin realised he was brushing away tears.

'That's not going to help you, crying.'

'Darry, if you knew the things I'd done for you . . . and Jade.'

'Don't make me laugh.'

'I mean it. I put my neck on the block to give her a clean break after Tulloch . . .'

'After Tulloch what?'

The phone line fell to silence.

For a moment, Fin stared at the screen willing himself to end the call but something stopped him. Darry needed to know, too. 'After . . . he raped her.'

They'd been friends for a long time, they'd grown up together, joined the army together. His mind was awash with memories of when they were children, the fights, the football, the girls. He returned to the phone, panic rising. 'I have money, lots of money. I took it for Jade, to y'know, help her get it sorted, you can have it.'

Darry stalled, the gap between them widening. 'We don't want your money.'

'Don't be stupid, think about what you're saying.'

'There's something I need more.'

'What, revenge? Is that it? Well you can't have it, he's gone, dead.'

'He might be, but you're not. Not yet anyway.'

'Darry, talk sense, man, please.'

'I'm perfectly sensible.'

232

'Come on, stop this . . .'
'Goodbye, Fin.'
The line died.
'Darry . . . Darry . . .'

41

DI Bob Valentine didn't bother to knock on Kyle Brogan's door this time, he merely turned the handle and walked in. DS McCormack closed the door behind them as Brogan appeared in the hallway, hands up like he was pleading with them not to shoot. He retreated two steps for every one the detectives took, talking all the while, without any coherence.

'Come on, Bob, I mean you're all in this together aren't you?' he said.

'I'm going to let you sit down and gather your thoughts before I say much more, Brogan.'

'What? I thought we were cool. I thought we'd sorted this out, I don't get this.'

McCormack had lost patience with Brogan too. 'Sit down and shut up. You'll speak when you're spoken to and if you don't say what we want to hear it'll be the last words you speak this side of a prison wall.'

Brogan eased himself into the sofa, dislodging the overloaded ashtray as he went. A landslide of cigarette ends fell to the floor. He reached out a hand, tried to stop the ash mountain in progress but his efforts had no effect, he sat back dusting his hands before finally resting his trembling fingers on his knees.

'That's better, Brogan,' said McCormack. The suspect's

eyes flitted left and right, he seemed confused by the DS's change of persona, like he was suddenly without support in the room. Even the flickering television, pitching surreal shadows at the walls, was on the officers' side.

'Now, what was that you were saying about giving a message to *my wee pal* . . . ?'

'Now look Mr Valentine, I'm sorry if I said the wrong thing.' Brogan's look spelled out his perplexity.

Valentine laughed aloud. 'I bloody well bet you are.'

'I wasn't trying to be wide with you, just y'know, having a bit of patter.'

'Oh, was that it? I see now. You'll have to forgive me, because the way I heard you say pass it on to *my wee pal*, I thought you must be . . .' he paused, then roared, 'assuming I was one of the bent coppers you're so familiar with.'

Brogan looked away. His Adam's apple rode up and down in his thin throat. He appeared to have lost some layers of skin, only an exposed and desperate soul was left.

'I'm not wrong, I see.' Valentine reached out for Brogan's vest and raised him from the sofa, his hands were two tight fists pressing on the thin man's chin.

'You're hurting my face.'

'Get used to it, the place you're going will make a sore face your best mate, you'll be begging for it just to get a break from having your arse split in two. Now I'm not messing here, Brogan, I've already told you this is a double murder investigation and I will run you in for it if you don't give me whatever it is you're holding, starting with the name of *my wee pal* on the force.'

'I can't . . . I told you everything I know.'

'That bullshit about the punch-up round the back of the Meat Hangers? How much bloody use is that going to be to me? I already have Tulloch and Finnie on my radar and I know why they were booted out the army so that amounts to squat all in my book.'

'Mr Valentine, you don't understand, this is bigger than me, I'd be on your books too if I say any more. I shouldn't even know what I do.'

The DI drew back a fist, he seemed ready to use it but McCormack stepped in, grabbing his arm. 'Let me take him down, sir. He might see sense in the cells.'

Valentine threw Brogan onto the sofa and stepped away, running his fingers through his hair like it might calm him down.

McCormack spoke: 'I'm guessing you had a visit from us after the Meat Hangers was stood over?'

'Aye. You know that.'

'I'm guessing it was one of Eddy Harris's team that came to see you?'

Valentine burst in. 'We bloody know who it was, we just need to hear him say it.'

'Aye and you've said that, what's in it for me, though?' said Brogan. 'I mean, if I stick my neck out you need to make it worth my while.'

'Am I hearing this? Are you seriously going on the make, here?' said Valentine. 'Because if you are, Brogan, I'll add that to the list of things I'm going to throw at you.'

'I'm saying, it's not easy, I'm in a position here . . .'

'He's scared, sir.'

'He should be. But not of Norrie Leask or Eddy Harris,

their days are over. Brogan, when I walk out that door, you're walking in front of me with your hands cuffed behind your back. Now, believe it or not, that's the facts. You're going down with all the rest of them, whether I decide to play up or play down your involvement is entirely up to you. You have one card, you're holding it, are you going to play it or are you going away for something like thirty years with the big boys.'

'I'm not one of the big boys, Mr Valentine.'

'I know that, Brogan, you're a scrote. A bottom feeder. A recidivist of low intelligence and lower character but if you run with the big dogs you're going to get some bloody big fleas. Now this is your last chance, Brogan, get onside with me and spare your mangy arse, or keep running with the pack that put you here.'

He stared at the television, his eyes widening and moistening. The options as Valentine had presented them appeared to have had an effect. Brogan slumped further into the sofa, his shoulders drooping towards the floor making his thin frame seem more rounded than it was. His breathing slowed, his thin lips and fragile mouth started to twitch at first, and then formed words. 'It was Eddy Harris. I'll make a statement if you want.'

Valentine caught McCormack smiling. He walked towards Brogan. 'When did he call?'

'I don't know, last week, after the break in some time.'

'You sound like he's a familiar face.'

'He's been around the club for years.' Brogan found a spark of energy, sat upright. 'I hope this is going in my favour.'

'Of course,' said Valentine. 'What do you mean Harris was around the club for years?'

'I don't know . . .'

'Come on, Brogan, you've only just started talking, don't ruin it for yourself.'

'I mean, I only know what I hear. Harris was always about the club, there'd been a bit of bother with dealers in the early days but Leask got them seen to by Harris. Leask had his own dealers who paid him a kickback, they were looked after by Harris and the others got punted.'

'So Eddy Harris was on Leask's payroll?'

'That's what they say. I mean, I'm sure he was, but not just for the stuff with the dealers. He was around a lot, too much, in the end. It was like Eddy had invested in the club or something, I don't know, he was in taking free drinks all the time and larging it up in the VIP suite. I don't know any more than that, I really don't, but I bet if you do some digging around you'll find more.'

'One last thing, Brogan, the night of the fight with Tulloch and Fin, was Eddy Harris around then?'

'Aye, I think he was. Yeah, I remember seeing him. I'm pretty sure he went upstairs with Leask and the others when the fight got stopped. But why do you ask?'

'I'm asking the questions, don't get above yourself.' Valentine nodded to McCormack. 'Get the bracelets on him, we need to get back to the station and sort this out.'

McCormack cuffed Brogan and sat him back on the sofa. Valentine was standing before the television, poised to switch it off as she approached. 'Sir, you don't really think Eddy's involved in this murder malarkey?

'Don't I?'

'Come on, he's just a bit flash, just a bent copper.'

'Sylvia, throughout this case the one thing I've consistently heard is *he's just* . . . he's just a scrote, he's just a squaddie, he's just a local hood. Let me tell you, there's something bigger than all of them going on here, it's gotten out of hand and made them all greater than the sum of their parts. Eddy Harris is involved, I don't know how but I will find out and when I do I'll hang him out to dry.'

Valentine reached forward to switch off the television.

'Hang on,' said McCormack.

'What?'

'Look, there on the news. It's the chief super.'

CS Marion Martin stood on the steps of King Street station with Major Rutherford and DI Eddy Harris. There was a sprinkling of uniform and some of the murder squad behind her, in front of her was a sheet of white paper which she prepared to read from, and the television cameras.

CS Martin spoke: 'Following the results of forensic testing today a woman has been arrested in relation to the murder of James Tulloch in his Ayrshire home. A report has been sent to the procurator fiscal detailing the evidence against Sandra Millar who is currently remanded in custody.'

'Am I hearing right? We've put Sandra Millar on a murder charge.'

Martin continued reading from her script a little while longer but the words became meaningless to Valentine. When she finished she dismissed the cameras with a brief 'no more questions' and was ushered inside by a fawning Major Rutherford.

'We've been screwed, Sylvia,' said Valentine. 'Bloody seriously screwed, and by our own side, too.'

42

As Valentine and McCormack arrived at King Street station the television staff were packing cameras into vans, winding up cables and collapsing tripods. Newspaper reporters called in their stories by phone whilst a few stray members of the public hovered about. It was an event for Ayr, if not one the town could be proud of.

Desk sergeant Jim Prentice looked up as Valentine entered the front foyer. 'Christ almighty, Bob, leave it on its hinges, eh!' he roared. 'Why are you barging in here leaving Incredible Hulk shapes in the door?'

Before he had a chance to respond DS McCormack arrived with Kyle Brogan in handcuffs, she presented him at the front desk and asked Jim to book him in.

'And what have you been up to this time, Brogan? Depriving toddlers of their lollipops again?'

'It's a stitch-up. I've done nowt.'

Valentine intervened, put an end to the speculation. 'Accessary to robbery, for now. If he pisses me off any more you can up it to accessory to murder.'

Brogan shook his head and kicked at the counter, his temper rising with his imminent confinement. 'You said you'd look after me.'

241

The desk sergeant spluttered a laugh. 'I hope you got that in writing, Brogan. Bob's got a tendency to let his mouth run away from him sometimes.'

'No he's right, Jim. I said I'd look after him, so will you put a cup of that dishwater we call tea in the cell with him.'

'You bastard!' yelled Brogan, but Valentine and McCormack had already moved off.

As the heavy fire door to the stairs clanged behind them Valentine imagined Jim cursing him once again, it was strange how proprietorial desk sergeants became towards the station, a form of institutionalisation no doubt. Days spent scribbling in a ledger and relaying the chief super's demands to officers she was too lazy to contact herself was no way to spend your life.

Climbing the stairs, the DI was certain he was about to put his job on the line. So what might his next role be? It might not even be on the force. Right now, that appealed to him.

'Slow down, sir,' said McCormack. 'You'll be too out of puff to speak your mind at this rate.'

'You're kidding aren't you? Dino's office could be on the top of Ben Nevis, I'd still be spewing by the time I got there.' He continued to pound the stairs, the slap of shoe-leather on the hard surface echoing loudly around him.

'Think about your heart,' yelled McCormack. 'You're not supposed to get overexcited.'

'Over excited, she can count herself lucky if I don't go off like a bloody Exocet missile.'

McCormack reached out and grabbed the detective by the hand. 'Bob, please, I'm saying this for you, calm down.'

Valentine looked at his hand, held tight in McCormack's, and jerked it away. It wasn't that he didn't want her to touch him, but that he was shocked by the sentiment, the obvious concern on show.

'I'm sorry, I didn't mean to upset you,' said McCormack.

'It's not that. I'm just more used to my warnings being shouted at me.'

'Shouting isn't going to solve anything.'

'That sounds like something I'd say to you.' He leaned against the wall and tugged at his tie, unbuttoned his collar. 'Look at me, getting all worked up.'

'You're the one that also told me Dino doesn't take confrontation well. I'm thinking about the case, too.'

'I'm sorry, Sylvia, I know everyone's put a lot of work in, it's just that you and I both know Sandra Millar didn't kill Tulloch.'

A brisk nod. 'It suits Dino, though, helps her clean-up rate and keeps the army sweet, avoids a whole bunch of trouble.'

'Ah, well . . .'

McCormack stepped back, steadied herself on the banister. 'Oh, Christ, you haven't told her about Phil and Ally's informant, have you?'

'I was going to do it today, after we'd seen Brogan. I didn't bloody well expect her to call a press conference the moment I stepped out the office.'

She rolled her gaze to the ceiling. 'Oh, God, it's going to be worse than I thought.'

'Don't worry about it. Just keep my back, all right?'

'I've always got your back.'

243

The DI proceeded to the chief super's office, his jaw clenched tight. There was a burning sensation rising from his stomach into his chest, like he'd tried to swallow something bitter, impossible to digest. As he reached the door and eyed the brassy nameplate, he halted and drew breath. His breathing was heavy now, he tried to find a steady pattern but it was impossible.

'Want me to knock?' said McCormack.

Valentine shook his head, raised his fist to the door, however before he got a chance to knock he heard peals of laughter on the other side – it was enough to prompt him to grab the handle and enter unannounced.

'Oh, hello, Bob.' CS Martin managed to attain her most smarmy demeanour in only three words. She didn't rise from behind her desk.

As Valentine gazed around the office he saw Major Rutherford sitting in front of Martin, a glass of something was perched on his knee, the ice inside rattled annoyingly. Eddy Harris sat nearby, looking a lot cockier than when Valentine had left him with a list of chores this morning. As the DI caught Harris's glare he nodded and spoke, raised a glass. 'Hello, Bob.'

Valentine withdrew his gaze but didn't reply, instead he approached the chief super's desk and leaned into her face. 'Sorry to interrupt your wee soirée but I think we should have a talk, in private.'

Martin's smile grew. 'I'm presuming you caught the lunchtime news, Bob.'

'You've made a very big mistake. Sandra Millar never killed anyone.'

'That's where you're wrong, Bob, we have the forensic evidence.' She reached for a blue folder on the edge of her desk. 'Read it and weep.'

'I don't care what it says, she didn't do it.'

Martin snatched back the folder, 'Look, the boffins found blood and tissue beneath the knife's handle, and some of it's Tulloch's. And they've successfully matched a partial print from the same handle to Sandra Millar, that sounds like a closed case to me, Bob.'

'Some of it? Are you saying Sandra Millar's isn't the only DNA on there?'

'It's enough to convict.'

'Well, maybe that's so, but I have specific evidence tying Tulloch to another suspect and testimony of police malpractice that I'd really like to raise with you in private, now, if you please.'

Martin's face changed shape, the smile slipped away. She peered over Valentine's shoulder towards DS McCormack. 'Are you in on this, Sylvia?'

'Yes, I am.'

'I had you down for a smart lassie as well,' said Martin. 'That doesn't require a reply ... And neither does your statement, Bob. Now, what exactly are you on about?'

Valentine pushed himself off the desk and addressed the others in the room too. 'If that's the way you want it then fine by me. It's probably better these two hear what I've learnt about them face to face anyway.'

Rutherford spoke: 'What's he saying?'

'Oh, come on, Tom,' said Valentine. 'You didn't really

think that I wouldn't find out about Tulloch and Finnie's discharge in such shady circumstances . . .'

Rutherford leaned forward, placed his glass on the desk but didn't speak.

Valentine turned to Martin. 'Alleged rape and murder of a civilian whilst on tour in Helmand Province, Afghanistan.'

'Not proven, I hasten to add,' said Rutherford.

'But presumably proven beyond the reasonable doubts of the regiment's top brass who punted them onto civvie street in a flash.'

CS Martin interrupted, 'What's all this about, Tom?'

'It's nothing, a silly coincidence.'

'It's no coincidence that Finnie registered complaints with us about Tulloch's stalking. Followed him around like a man with a grudge, even took a job in the same nightclub and picked a fight with him.' Valentine was enjoying watching Rutherford's reaction.

'Is this true?' said Martin.

'Well, there's truth and there's stretching the *actualité*,' said Rutherford.

Martin got out of her seat and walked to the other side of the desk. 'Is this true? Did you kick them out of the army after a civilian rape and murder investigation?'

'Well, that might, strictly speaking, be true but don't you see it's how he's dressing it up?'

Valentine replied, 'Major, I'm a police officer, my strong suit isn't dressing things up. You must be confusing me with our friends on the press, who I'm sure will be able to embroider the *actualité* without my assistance.'

'Oh, bloody hell,' said Martin. She turned to Valentine.

246

'And try not to sound so bloody smug about it, Bob. I can't believe you're just coming to me with this now, you must have known beforehand.'

'They were very serious allegations, I had to have them verified.' Valentine watched Harris sink further into his seat, he seemed to be wishing himself somewhere else. 'A bit like the police malpractice, I mentioned. Yes, you'd do well to squirm, Eddy. You see, DI Harris has been taking back-handers from Norrie Leask for some time.'

'Now wait a minute,' said Harris.

'Shut up, Eddy,' said Martin, 'let him finish.'

'You see, Eddy here has been ferreting away a nice little bundle from the very same club where both Tulloch and Finnie worked and where he has himself been investigating a very interesting robbery.'

'What's the Meat Hangers got to do with the murders?' said Martin.

'Maybe Eddy can enlighten us, since he's been on Norrie Leask's payroll for such a long time.'

'Where did you get this bullshit?' said Harris.

'I wouldn't call it bullshit,' said Valentine. 'We have an employee ready to testify.'

'Who?'

'Kyle Brogan.'

Harris tutted. 'Don't make me laugh, bungling Brogan's a scrote, what court's going to believe him?'

Valentine knew Brogan was the weak link in the case, he withdrew himself to the rim of the desk and folded his arms. 'Normally I would agree, Eddy. But, you see, when you have the accountant's ledger too and the accountant deciphering the list of payments made to you from Leask I'd say that strengthens my hand a little.'

Martin spoke up, she addressed no one in particular. 'Is this true?'

'Yes, chief, it's true,' said McCormack. 'I interviewed the accountant, a Mr Bullough, who has operated from premises in Barns Street for more than twenty years. He's ready to testify for us, too.'

Harris's shoulders slumped forward, pitching him on the edge of his chair. He stared at the carpet, as if he was hoping a hole would appear that he could dive into.

'Now he's slightly more reliable than Brogan, proper letters after his name and everything,' said Valentine. 'I'm sure that's good enough for the courts, don't you think, Eddy?'

43

Darry Millar sat in the Ardrossan ferry terminal and watched Jade collect two teas from the little kiosk. The woman with the tabard and the bad perm who was serving seemed to be eying Jade up and down, she'd be from the island, people tended to have a strange view of mainlanders on Arran. When his sister returned he took the styrofoam cup and started to blow on the top of the greying liquid.

'Looks like shit,' said Jade.

'Bet it doesn't taste much better, but beggars can't be choosers, can they?'

They sat in silence for a moment, watched the day-trippers and tourists arriving, there were backpackers and wealthier middle-aged couples who had left their BMWs in the car park, preferring not to risk a scratch or two on the ferry crossing.

'Why Arran, Darry?'

'We need to get away for a bit.'

Jade grimaced as she tasted the tea, placed the cup on the floor beside her chair leg. 'You say that like we're going on holiday too.'

'It's not going to be a holiday, Jade. Far from it,' said Darry. 'I've got unfinished business with Fin, I told you that.'

'You don't even know he's there.'

'He's there.'

'How do you know that?'

'Because when I spoke to him on your phone I heard the sound of the ferry horn, I couldn't mistake it.'

'That could have been anywhere.'

'It was Arran, I knew he'd go there. I know just the spot, the bothy we used to camp in when we were kids, we even stayed there when we came here with the army, the regiment all had proper billets but Fin wanted to go to the bothy, he's sentimental like that. Won't feel so bloody nostalgic about the place when I get a hold of him, mind.'

Jade got to her feet. 'I'm sick of hearing about you and Fin. Since when was any of this just about the pair of you?' She turned from Darry and stamped towards the ferry exit, as she went her foot connected with the tea cup and sent it spilling across the floor.

'Jade, wait up . . .' Darry picked up his things and ran after his sister, splashing through the spilled tea.

He found her in the bar on the top deck, staring out at the open waters. She looked forlorn, like she was thinking about the past, or worse, the future.

'Found you at last . . .' He put the newspaper he'd bought and a chocolate bar on the table behind her.

'Had to be somewhere.'

'Suppose.' The ferry was leaving port, people crammed themselves into the bolted-down tables and chairs, it was busy but not as packed as the peak season. Darry offered his sister the chocolate, she declined and he joined her staring out at the sea. 'I used to love coming over here.

Going to the castle in Brodick and climbing Goatfell, it's a beautiful little place.'

'It looks miserable today.' Jade stared out the window.

'It might pick up when we get there.' He was ashamed by the triteness of his remark. He knew it wasn't a pleasure cruise, it wasn't even a proper escape from all they'd been through. It was a detour that he had to take to sort out something personal before he could even think about helping Jade get her own life back to normality.

'No it won't pick up.' Jade turned away from the window, started to flick through the *Evening Times*.

Darry placed a hand on the cover, 'Stop that. I want to talk to you.'

A huff. 'What about now?'

'Look, if you can stop being so teenage for a moment and tell me what happened, y'know, on the night Jim died. I really need to know.'

'I am teenage. And he was murdered, don't you read the papers?'

'Jade, please. I need everything straight in my head before we see Fin.'

'I don't know what you want me to say, I wasn't there when it happened.'

Darry pressed his weight onto his elbows, the table-top was strong enough to stay firm. 'You were thereabouts, you were home before it all kicked off.'

'I don't want to talk about it anymore.'

'Jade, I do. If we're ever going to get Mum back and get this mess cleaned up then we're going to have to do a damn sight more talking about the events of that night.'

She put her face in her hands, shook her head. When she spoke, it came in a slow, childish droll. 'Jim got home, and there was a row. Mum was screaming at him and he was laughing and teasing her, I think she knew or guessed about me. She'd been asking me what was wrong for long enough, what with all the crying and moods and everything, she must have guessed.'

'Are you sure, Jade? I mean, they'll ask about that in court or whatever.'

She nodded. 'He . . . he said I was a little slag, that we were all little whores in the end and Mum, she . . . She started to hit him. I couldn't hear everything properly after that, they went into the kitchen. I heard her screaming and screaming at him, and when her voice rose she said he was a liar and she wanted him out of her house and that she didn't know what she ever saw in him.' Jade started to weep.

'You're doing fine, keep going.'

'There was some stuff about Dad, nasty stuff that Jim said but Mum wouldn't let him. I think she attacked him with something then, I don't know what, a pan maybe, something metal because it clanged on the ground afterwards. There was a lot of noise, a lot of screaming after that, but I never heard Jim's voice again. Then Mum ran out.'

'Where were you?'

'I was outside by then, I ran out. I stayed over the road, it was raining and dark. I saw Mum stumble into the wall, then she fell in the garden. I couldn't look, I just buried my face in my hands and wanted it all to go away, but then that old bat from the house across the road appeared, she said something to Mum and I just ran. I wanted it to be all over, I didn't want to think. I just ran away and sat under a tree trying to block it all out. I didn't move. I didn't do anything until the police came . . . and that's when I called you.'

Darry sat quietly. He watched Jade sobbing and wiped the tears from her cheeks. 'You've done well, Jade. You don't need to tell me any more.'

'Darry, I know you blame Fin now, but you shouldn't.'

'That's enough, Jade. You don't know what you're talking about.'

'I do, you think he should have been looking out for me but he couldn't be there every minute of the day. Fin was good to me, he said he would help, said he would help me get this sorted.' She rubbed her stomach. 'He said he'd pay for it and make sure that we could get away and start again if we had to.'

Darry turned around the newspaper, flicked the pages. 'Stop now, Jade. You don't understand, if it wasn't for Fin then Jim Tulloch would never have been anywhere near us. He was a psychopath and Fin brought him into our home, he followed Fin to Ayr, and that's what all this mess is about – Jim's twisted revenge for something that happened in Afghanistan. Fin has wrecked our family, Mum's in hospital, you were raped for Christ's sake, Jade. A friend should never have let that happen, and he was supposed to be my friend.'

'You're just looking for someone to blame, you're angry and want to hit out. In a while, Darry, you'll calm down and see that this was nothing to do with Fin.'

Darry fell silent, stared at the newspaper spread out on the table in front of him. He didn't listen to Jade, because whatever she said it wouldn't change the monumental news looking back at him from the pages of the newspaper.

'Darry, do you hear me?'

He looked up from the tabletop. His eyes were glazed over, like he had just wakened from sleep.

'Darry, what is it?'

He turned back to the newspaper and flipped the page over for Jade to see what he had just read. 'It's Mum, she's been charged with the murder.'

'They can't.'

'There.' He tapped at the page. 'It says so in the paper.' His eyes closed. 'It says they have evidence she killed Tulloch.'

44

DI Eddy Harris raised his face to the ceiling, closed his eyes. He appeared to be awaiting divine intervention or at least a lifeline from the chief super: neither appeared. With each second that ticked away it seemed the room became more claustrophobic, like the walls closed in and the oxygen supply was depleted.

Valentine's gaze flitted between Harris and the others, everyone was staring at Harris, waiting for a response to the allegation he'd been paid by Leask. Could it be true? Could a police officer, even one like Flash Harris, really be so stupid? 'Nothing to say for yourself, Eddy?'

He opened his eyes. 'Nothing that changes the situation.'

CS Martin slapped the heel of her hand on the desktop. 'You'll have to do a damn sight better than that, Eddy, or I'll pick up the phone and reserve a nice cell for you downstairs, one with hot and cold running recrimination. Don't think about saving your job, think about saving your skin because without some mitigation in your defence I'm throwing the book at you.'

Major Rutherford started to rise from his seat, he looked like he wanted to be invisible too. 'I don't think you need me here for this, Marion. I'll see myself out.'

'You'll sit your arse down,' said Martin. 'As soon as I'm

finished with him, you're up next. And if I need Home Office approval to see those case files on Tulloch and Finnie, I'll get it, along with a warrant for your arrest on charges of impeding a murder investigation which resulted in the death of a minor. Am I making myself clear enough, *Tom?*'

'But, but . . . Look this is silly, we have the case tied up.'

'No buts!' Martin blasted. 'You have made me look a bloody muppet today, and on television too. I won't forget that in a long time. If you think I'm going to let you slither off back to barracks and forget your involvement, think again.' She moved in front of Harris, pointed a finger in his face. 'Now spill your guts from start to finish, Eddy, or so help me God I'll make you such a poster boy for bent coppers that they'll be writing you into the textbooks.'

Harris gathered his breath and looked about the room as if surveying the exits. If he was thinking of making a dash for the door he declined and spoke up instead. 'What do you want to know?'

'Everything,' said the chief super.

Valentine prompted him. 'How about you confirm the robbery was planned by Leask and that you knew all about it.'

'Now come on, Bob . . .'

'No, you come on. I have statements confirming you were there when Leask put up the job.' He was stretching the facts again, but time was running out and there'd never be another opportunity where the pressure on Harris was so intense.

Harris leaned forward, spoke to his hands: 'There was a

256

punch-up between the pair of them, it'd been on the cards for some time but Leask let it fester because he wanted them for the job – they were ex-army so it was like hiring proper professionals. He liked that idea, didn't want any balls-ups, you see.'

'Go on,' said Valentine.

'He hauled them in after the fight, made them think they were both getting the bullet from the Meat Hangers, but then drew it back.'

'Made them an offer they couldn't refuse, you mean?'

'He said if they staged the robbery that they could keep their jobs and that he'd put a good drink in it for them too.'

'And they went for it just like that?'

'No. Not at first. That's where I came in, we agreed to stage the robbery on one of my shifts so I could make sure the investigation ignored them.'

'You bloody idiot, Eddy.'

Martin turned around, she folded her arms as she stared out the window of her office. 'How much was in it for you?'

'From the robbery, nothing. Honestly, I never took a thing.'

'Oh, come on . . .'

'No, I'm serious. I never took any because I was just protecting my investment, if the Meat Hangers went under then I did too. I couldn't stay afloat now without the money Leask feeds me, I'm a bloody fool, I know, but I didn't have a choice, I've got debts up to my eyeballs.'

It was an old story and one that Valentine had heard too many times already to summon an ounce of sympathy. He had financial difficulties of his own but he had never been tempted to put his fingers in the till. 'So, what went wrong? Tulloch and Fin screwed Leask I take it?'

'I don't know, and that's the God's honest.' Harris looked up from the floor and pleaded, 'I didn't know there was going to be a murder, Bob, I'd never have got involved with anything like that, I swear to it.'

'Well something went tits up.'

'Yes, big time. But don't ask me what. All I know is the money went missing and Leask went ballistic.'

'He also went missing,' said Valentine.

Martin responded, 'Where's Leask now?'

'I don't know,' said Eddy.

'Don't tell me you don't know. Tell me you do know or you'll find out and have the answer with me in under a minute or I'll throw you to the wolves, Eddy.'

'He could be anywhere,' said Harris. 'I suspected the Paton boy was his work too. I called him on it and he admitted Joe had gone too far. Supposedly it was an accident, Joe being over-exuberant trying to get information about where the money was, but after that I was out. I broke off all communication. Jesus Christ, I'm a police officer, maybe not a good one, but I know the consequences of where this is all going.'

'Do you, Eddy?' said Martin. 'I don't think you've the faintest idea.' She picked up the telephone and threw it in his lap. 'Get onto Leask now, get a whereabouts and get bloody moving.'

As Harris dialled the number the office fell into silence. Valentine tried to weigh up what he had just seen and heard but it was almost too much for him. Eddy had been a fool but could he judge him for that? Every day he himself had dealt with people like Norrie Leask and faced temptation, all it took was a brief loss of concentration or even carelessness and you were in the drink. Valentine was lucky to be a family man – his wife and daughters meant everything to him – but others weren't so fortunate to have what he did. If Harris had slipped up and Leask had found out then the chances were that he would do anything Leask asked to keep quiet. People were simple to handle when they had secrets. When they were vain and stupid too, like Harris, then they were easy to manipulate.

Harris replaced the receiver on the cradle and looked towards the chief super. 'That was Joe.'

'Who?' she said.

'Leask's wingman, he takes care of business, well most business.'

'He's a wrist breaker, a raving psycho,' said Valentine. 'Stop stalling, Eddy, where's Leask?'

'Well, the last place I expected – Brodick.'

'He's on Arran?' said Martin.

'Dining in fine style as we speak, at the Auchrannie Hotel.'

'What the bloody hell's he doing there?'

'Seems he got a tip-off. He's been looking for Grant Finnie, or more precisely he's been looking for his money, Finnie just happens to be in possession of it.'

'Well he won't be for much longer if Leask has his way,' said Valentine.

The chief super reached into her drawer and pulled out her car keys, threw them at Valentine. 'That's all we need another murder to add to the two, now unsolved, we already have. Try explaining that to the bloody papers.'

'What am I to do with these?' said Valentine, holding up the keys.

'Get driving.' She was putting on her jacket, heading for the door. 'We can't leave this to the island plod, it's a potential murder not a missing bobble hat.'

'We'll need to get the ferry, preferably one that takes vehicles.'

'Shit. Tell me this isn't happening.'

Valentine moved towards the desk, stretched over and pulled the phone towards him. 'I'm calling Glasgow, get them to send the copter.'

Martin dug her hands into her jacket pockets, leaned her back against the wall and sighed to the heavens. 'Blow my budget as well, why don't you . . . Get onto the Air Support Unit in Glasgow now, Bob.'

45

Valentine directed the helicopter controller at Air Support to collect himself, Martin and McCormack from the Low Green and called ahead for uniform to make sure the area was cleared. There was only one helicopter under contract to the force and he had expected a protracted debate about its usage but got none after offering the controller the opportunity to speak with CS Martin personally. He smiled at the response, but didn't let on why; the chief super had started pacing her office now, breaking into occasional rants at DI Harris and Major Rutherford.

'I should put the bloody pair of you in the cells, now,' said CS Martin. 'Just about pushed me out the door to front that press conference didn't you? It'll be a long time before I live that down.'

As she berated the men, Valentine confirmed the details once more with Air Support and stepped away from the phone. 'Right, we'll set off in ten minutes,' he said.

'What's wrong with right away?' said Martin.

Valentine flagged her down. 'We've got plenty of time, they have to get here first.'

The CS took the opportunity to start once more on the list of grievances she had with Harris and Rutherford.

261

'Sylvia, get Phil and Ally in here would you, they can escort this pair of twats down to the interview rooms and make a start on getting full statements.'

'Hang on a minute,' said Rutherford. 'I don't think you've got any cause to hold me here.'

'Don't you? Well that's good I don't give a bloody toss what you think, Tom. But if you're looking for a reason to hang around then how about a detailed account of why you saw fit to withhold vital information from my officers relating to Tulloch and Finnie.'

'I hardly think it was vital . . .'

'A boy died, a sixteen-year-old because you wrong-footed my team, or doesn't that bother you? No probably not, just another bit of collateral damage in your campaign isn't it?'

Sylvia broke in, 'Phil and Ally are on their way up right away.'

'Good,' said Martin. 'Tell them to contact the Ministry of Defence with the new facts and get all the case files relating to Tulloch and Finnie's departure from the army. I want to see heads roll. We're going to blow this cover-up wide open.'

Valentine took the driver's seat of Martin's Audi. The road to the Low Green passed mainly in silence, except for the chief super's curses every time a traffic light shone red or a pedestrian dared to cross in front of the car. There was very little she could say to mend the situation, an apology would be trite and useless, and wouldn't bring back the murder victims or those who had been affected by their deaths. Saying sorry might be some kind of balm to Valentine's ego, but he didn't want to hear it; he knew Martin was, if not contrite, then feeling an embarrassment verging on shame and that was good enough for him.

'Sir, would you like me to call ahead, tell the local officers we're on the way?' said McCormack.

'God no,' said Valentine. 'You'll only scare the horses. Or worse, the local team will wade in and we'll be chasing Leask through the wilds for the next fortnight. No, they can find out why we're there when we arrive.'

'Yes, sir.'

At the Low Green the team caught the sound of the helicopter in the distance, a few day-trippers were interested enough to stop and stare at the sky. Uniform were clearing the ground for landing, herding people onto the pavements and stopping dog walkers from heading for the grass. As they waited, counting the moments to the copter's descent, Martin approached Valentine and said, 'This is a bloody mess, isn't it?'

'It's not pretty.'

'I'll get my knuckles reddened for this, you know.'

'I don't think you can be blamed.'

Martin spat, 'No. And neither do I, Bob, but we both know that's not going to stop them.'

'I suppose not,' he dipped his head. 'But you shouldn't blame yourself.'

She calmed for a moment, then resumed her talk. 'Tell me, did you suspect Eddy of anything, ever?'

The chief super gazed into Valentine, he saw she was checking him for non-verbal cues that might betray him so he held firm. Harris was finished, he knew that, and there was very little to be gained from making matters any worse for him. Despite the situation, the DI saw that Harris didn't need any more trouble. 'No, I never suspected Eddy of anything.'

'No, me neither. His coat's been on a slack hook for a long time but I thought that was him just getting lazy – turns out he's been anything but. Silly bastard. He'll be hung out to dry for this.'

'And so he should be.' It didn't please Valentine to think of another officer being brought down, even Flash Harris. But an officer treating the job with such contempt, that was something altogether different. He couldn't imagine letting his own standards fall so low, how could anyone else? There was a collective shame that Harris had brought on everyone and Valentine didn't want to see others in the station suffer because of it.

The noise of the downdraught and the whirring blades of the helicopter curtailed their conversation. As the copter's side-doors opened the team piled in and fastened themselves into their seats for the short journey across the Firth of Clyde. The pilot motioned them to put on their earphones and then relayed the message that they were landing on a playing field in Brodick, it was approximately half a mile from the hotel where Leask was staying.

Valentine turned to the pilot. 'Call ahead when we're a few minutes from landing and get a squad car to pick us up.'

'If I can find anyone, the place isn't fully manned.'

'Brilliant. Let's hope there's nothing serious going down, like a goat in labour.'

The small island started to hove into view. The bright blues of sky and sea butting gently with the lush greens and deeper browns of the land and hills. It seemed a jagged, dramatic place. The cliff crags and the jutting peaks appearing starkly in contrast to the mainland's built-up conformity.

'It's beautiful,' said DS McCormack.

'Don't tell me you've never been to Arran,' said Valentine.

'Never. It's so wild and harsh, yet peaceful.'

'They call it Scotland in miniature ... and all life is here.'

The helicopter seemed to swing out to sea again and then backed up on itself and drifted closer to the coast. They were now near enough to see people looking up to the skies and the branches of trees bending downwards in the rotor's wake. The pilot waved to a man on the ground who was standing by a pair of red cones, flagging his hands above his head. The engines heaved a last loud burst and then the helicopter was lowered to the ground, the wheels bouncing gently and then staying still.

The blades above were still turning as the squad got out. A man in uniform, holding his hat pressed tight to his head, approached.

'Inspector Valentine?' he said.

'Yes, that's me.' The DI introduced the others and the uniform announced himself as DS Rory McNeil.

'If you follow me,' he said. 'I have a car waiting to take you round to the Auchrannie . . . it's the Astra estate over there.'

'That would be the big white one with *police* on the side?'

'I see there's little gets past you, sir.'

At the hotel Valentine instructed DS McNeil to drop them some distance from the front entrance. 'I don't want to tip off Leask, if it can at all be helped.'

At the front desk a young girl in a black jacket, her name tag on the lapel, greeted them with a smile. CS Martin frowned and produced her warrant card. 'Police. I think you better call your duty manager.'

The girl's gaze fell on the telephone, she picked up the receiver. 'Erm, he's not answering.'

'We need to remove a guest, right away.'

'Remove?'

'The sooner the better. Can you tell me what room Norrie Leask is in?'

The girl was unsure of herself but went to the computer, tapped a few keys. 'Mr Leask is in Room 212.'

'What about his companion?'

'Is that Joe Barr? . . . He's in the next room 214. We don't have any rooms with the number 13 in them.'

'Well that's lucky,' said Martin. 'Sylvia, grab the lassie's jacket and a tray, you're going to deliver some room service to Mr Leask.'

'I'm not sure if I can do that,' said the receptionist.

'Trust me, you can. Or would you prefer to keep a murder suspect upstairs?'

The officers headed for the lift. Once outside Leask's

door, Valentine stationed himself to the left of the spy hole and CS Martin stood outside room 214.

'OK, Sylvia, knock-knock . . .'

McCormack tapped on the door and called out, 'Room service.'

No answer.

'Knock again,' said Valentine.

Another knock, harder this time.

'OK. OK. I'm coming.' The voice behind the door was a middle-aged man's, heavy Ayrshire in tone.

'Soon as the chain's off, kick it in,' said Valentine.

The door opened, the chain wasn't on. McCormack kicked the door in and Norrie Leask fell backwards into the room, cursing.

'Stay where you are, Norrie,' said Valentine.

The sound of footsteps padded from the interior of the room to the front door where the officers waited.

'You too, Joe. This is a bit like a full house,' said Valentine. 'In here, chief.'

As Martin came in McCormack was cuffing Leask behind his back, propping him against the wall. Valentine was turning the protesting Joe around. 'Just shut it, now. You'll have plenty of time to tell us all about it when we get you down the nick.'

'It's not us you want,' said Leask.

'You'll do for now,' said McCormack.

'But they're here,' said Leask. 'You're letting them get away . . .'

CS Martin stepped towards Leask. 'What is he going on about?'

Before Leask had a chance to reply DS McNeil appeared at the doorway. 'I just had a call on the radio, I think you should hear this – there's been shots fired out at the old bothy in Glen Rosa.'

'I told you,' wailed Leask. 'You got the wrong ones.'

'Shut it, Norrie.' said Valentine. 'Where's this Glen Rosa?'

46

Valentine led Leask through the hotel foyer to the car park. A few guests in gym wear, obviously en route to the leisure club, stopped and stared but were promptly waved aside. As McNeil arrived with the second custody and CS Martin, Valentine was putting Leask in the back of the Astra, a wary hand on the top of his head as he ducked the roof.

'How are we all going to get in there?' said Valentine.

'We need the Land Rover for the glen, it's on the way with our armed response officer,' said McNeil.

'You have armed response on Arran?'

'Not exactly. We have a couple of rifles, and my offsider has them in the Land Rover for the odd stray deer, we get them on the roads and they can do terrible damage to a vehicle.' He put Joe in the back of the Astra with Leask, where he rattled his handcuffs and continued to protest.

'I'll go with uniform to keep an eye on this pair,' said DS McCormack.

Valentine nodded, turned back to McNeil – he wanted to know more about the guns. 'Tell me you have the proper firearms training.'

'Of course. Have to, as you know . . .'

'And have you actually fired one?'

'Oh, yes. I shot a cow once, had been hit by a post van and was in a dreadful way, blood oozing out the nose, the tongue lolling . . .'

Thank you for the image,' said Valentine.

'The kindest thing for it was to put it out of its misery.'

The DI turned to the chief super. 'I'd love to see the paperwork on that.'

'Oh, jeez, you wouldn't have liked to fill it in,' replied McNeil. 'The best part of a day it took me, I had to reload a few times you see. I suppose I was lucky it wasn't a built-up area, now that would have been a nightmare.'

The conversation halted abruptly as the Land Rover appeared and a uniformed officer opened the door and got out. The CS and the DI piled in as McNeil directed the uniform towards DS McCormack and the awaiting collars in the back seat of the Astra.

'Come on, Rory, you have to drive us there. We're wasting time,' said Martin.

As he got behind the steering wheel McNeil detailed the route. Glen Rosa was a scenic spot on the edge of Brodick with a rambling track to the top of the Goatfell range. It could be boggy in places but there were beaten-earth tracks that the Land Rover could handle easily if it came to that.

'There's a wee road leads there, just outside Brodick, we'll be there in no time,' said McNeil.

'What's the story with the shots?' said Martin.

'There's a campsite, with an old stone bothy, I think the campers use it as a washroom now. There was a call, shots were heard inside. Some voices, screams but nobody's seen anything, we'll be the first on the scene, I'm afraid. Can you handle a rifle, chief super?'

'No I bloody cannot. And nor do I intend to.'

'No worries. Sure, I'm a bit of an action man myself and Bob there looks the part.'

As they travelled, Valentine's mind flushed with previous similar encounters. There had never been gunshots, only knives, but one of those had found its way through the walls of his heart and he wasn't keen to repeat the experience. The pain had been inconsequential compared to the hurt it had caused his family, he couldn't bring himself to think about Clare or the girls having to go through that again. He forced away his fears.

'How the hell did it come to this?' said Martin.

Did she mean an armed stand-off on Arran? Or, the pair of them sitting in a car heading for their potential doom? 'Well, we were short-staffed before you bumped Harris.'

'I've a bloody good mind to go and get him, send him in there now.'

Valentine agreed. 'We could all march behind him, let Flash Harris do the talking.'

'He's used to shooting his mouth off, he wouldn't need a gun.'

The Land Rover came screeching to a halt in a gravel road, spraying scree beyond the tyres and jerking the occupants in their seats.

'Right, we're here,' said McNeil.

Valentine was first out of the vehicle. He spotted a small group of tourists and campers gathered beyond a dry-stone dyke; the DI observed them for a few seconds then summoned them away from the wall. The group trailed slowly towards him and as McNeil appeared with the rifles those in front of him increased their pace.

'Get inside that house.' Valentine pointed to a whitewashed cottage; the group stalled, some were ready to question but he blasted, 'Move!'

As the officers descended the path towards the bothy, Valentine rebuffed the offer of a rifle and DS McNeil continued on with one gun strapped over each shoulder.

'I don't want you to fire that unless it's a matter of life and death, is that clear?' said the DI.

'Yes, sir.'

The path was narrow and rutted. Gnarled roots from adjacent trees impeded the way and a damp covering from earlier rain made the going slippy underfoot. As he reached the corner of the bothy Valentine directed McNeil towards a gap in the adjoining fence where he could reach a rusting plough for cover, he jogged on and signalled a thumbs up to say he had secured a view of the open doorway.

'Christ this is hardcore, Bob,' said Martin.

'You're not kidding.'

'If I'd known we were going to end up playing commandos in the wilds I'd have packed the Kevlar vests.'

'Bet you didn't imagine we'd be doing this when you sat down to your cornflakes this morning?'

'No I did not. If I had, it wouldn't have been milk I was splashing on them, I can assure you of that.' Martin wiped some mud splashes away from the elbow of her jacket. 'Right, what are you thinking?'

'I'm going to make my way round the building, when I get close enough to the open door at the front I'm going to try and engage with them.'

'That's your plan, is it?'

'Got a better one?'

She narrowed her gaze towards the bothy. 'Sit tight and wait for the proper back-up.'

'Not an option. It's going to be dark in about forty minutes, there's potentially a hostage or two in there, we can't take the risk.'

She baulked, 'And this isn't a risk?'

Valentine didn't answer. He crouched below the line of the window on the bothy's gable end and started to feel his way around the outside of the building, his heart ramped and a damp line of sweat formed on his forehead. As he turned he spotted the chief super with the back of her head resting on the wall, eyes skywards; he hoped she was praying.

The DI heard movement inside the building, he tried to assess the number of people but it was impossible. There were words, a man's voice, he seemed to be pleading, his tone rising and falling with increasing desperation. There was also crying, it sounded like a woman's voice, or perhaps a young girl's.

As he reached the open doorway of the bothy Valentine peered round the edge, ignoring that a bullet might meet him. The interior was in almost complete darkness, only a little light coming in from the small case and sash window on the other side of the building. When the sun finally receded, the place would be in complete darkness. From his own knowledge of bothies, there wasn't likely to be an electric light source. If there was, surely they would have used it by now. He reasoned that it was unlikely they had candles or a torch and so darkness was definitely a fast approaching possibility. With a gun in the room, and a jumpy, captive party, the consequences of any attempt to use the diminishing light as cover could be tragic.

Valentine positioned himself on his haunches, started to remove his jacket and tie; the pinstripe jacket was a present from Clare that made him long for his family. As he rolled up the sleeves, folded the jacket away, he hoped he'd be putting it on again soon. At the doorway the DI leaned in – his only hope was establishing contact as quickly as possible. 'Hello, can I have your attention, please . . .'

There was no reply.

'My name is Detective Inspector Bob Valentine of Police Scotland . . . can we talk, please?'

The reply was direct, roared straight from the gut: 'Go to hell!'

'I'm afraid that's not going to be an option, not immediately anyway.'

'I'm warning you, bugger off now or you'll regret it.' The voice belonged to a young man, his accent was not as pronounced as Leask's had sounded back at the hotel, but it was definitely Ayrshire.

'Am I talking to Grant Finnie?'

The same voice replied. 'No. I told you to do one, now get lost.'

Movement, bodies shuffling towards the door, was heard inside. Another voice shouted, 'He has a gun.'

'Grant, stop it,' a young girl screamed. 'He'll shoot again, don't . . . don't.'

'You're bloody right I'll use it, get back.'

The noise of shuffling feet came again, then the interior was lit with a flash and gunshot blasted off the walls.

'Don't shoot,' yelled Valentine. 'Please, put the gun down, we can talk this through without the gun.'

The girl's tears sounded heavier now, a confusion of voices moved inside the bothy. Scuffles, shoes scraping on hard, bare floors. A tense rush towards the deeper recesses of the building followed.

'There's nothing to talk about,' the man's voice came again, this time Valentine deduced it was a maddened Darry Millar. 'All the talking's been done.'

'Darry, come on, put down the gun and come outside. We can sort this out, it's not too late, trust me.'

'Trust you? You're bloody filth, where were you when my sister was raped? Same place my supposed best mate was, nowhere to be seen.'

Finnie spoke up: 'Darry, I told you, I did all I could. I said I'd sort it and I did.'

'How? She's pregnant, that bastard raped her and now she's having his baby.'

Jade's tears became hysterical, broke into deep sobs. 'Stop it. Stop it. Stop it.'

'But he paid, didn't he?' said Finnie.

'He paid and the filth have my mother for it, she's going to get put away for that bastard.'

Valentine tried to intervene again, the situation was slipping out of control. The men inside the bothy were agitated and the girl was getting hysterical. 'Darry, you've got it all wrong. Now come on, give me the gun and let us talk this through properly.'

'Shut it, filth!' He fired the gun again, this time the shot left the building, leaving a burst of smoke evacuating through the doorway with it.

The DI looked out into the ebbing light, he saw CS Martin peering round the corner, she was frantically waving her arms about, flagging him to withdraw, begging a retreat. He turned away. Beyond the path leading to the mountain ranges he saw the last bursts of daylight chinking in the burn. It was a beautiful sight, in the blue-black sky above, the winding waters and the humped backs of the hills. There were worse places to die. He stood up and headed for the doorway, leaving behind the hard breathing and heavy pounding of his heart that had kept him back.

As Valentine marched into the bothy and faced Darry Millar the gun was levelled at his heart.

'You want some of this?' said Darry.

'What good's that going to do you?' said Valentine. 'More importantly, what good's that going to do Jade?'

'I'm warning you, I'll shoot.'

'Darry, think about it.' The strength of his voice emboldened him. 'You're all she's got now, don't make this any worse for Jade. If you get put away she's got nobody.'

Jade called out. 'Listen to him. Darry put down the gun.'

'I'm in charge here, I'll decide what happens with the gun.' He walked towards Finnie, pushing the gun in his face. 'I trusted you like you were my own brother. You said you'd look after Jade. She didn't have a dad, only me. You were supposed to be there for her . . .'

'I was. You don't understand.'

'You and Tulloch, eh, what really went on in Helmand? Why did you really get punted out of the army? The pair of you, like best mates together.'

'No. It wasn't like that, you know that. He followed me to Ayr, he blamed me because I reported him. He did it in Helmand too, but the girl was shot, everyone knew it . . . Even you knew it, how can you pretend otherwise?'

'I don't know what I know anymore. I lost everything the night Jade called to say Tulloch was dead. I took off that night, ran out on the army, because somebody had to sort it, but I couldn't because he'd already raped her. I was too late . . . and now look at the mess.'

'But I sorted it for you, Darry. Can't you even see that? I sorted everything.'

'She was wandering the streets, crying. Look at her, still crying. She's cried every day since because she can't see my mother and now she never will. The mother we knew died that night too. She killed Tulloch but do you think the courts will care why?'

'She didn't kill him,' said Finnie.

'She did. Read the papers, it's there in black and white . . . They have her locked up already.'

'She didn't kill Tulloch. I did,' said Finnie.

Darry lowered the gun, it shook in his hand. 'What did you say?'

'It was me, not your mother . . . I killed Tulloch.'

Jade wiped her eyes and ran to her brother, held him in

277

her arms. Her grip squeezed the anger from Darry, he stood limply, like he might now be the one to fall without his sister's support.

'I killed Tulloch,' said Finnie again. 'Your mother stuck a knife in his back but he was still alive, still breathing, moving – I finished him like they showed us. I sorted everything, you see, for all of us.'

Darry turned towards Valentine. 'What's he going on about, it said in the paper you had charged Mum?'

'That should never have happened, son.' The DI held out a hand, stepped forward. 'Come on, he's confessed now, you can get your mum back.'

Darry dropped the pistol to the stone floor – Valentine was close enough to lunge and retrieve the Luger. He backed away again, turned and removed the magazine. As he stuck the gun in his belt he faced Darry and Jade again and motioned them to the door.

The brother and sister moved together, gripping each other separately, but somehow as part of the same crawling mass of limbs. They were both wounded and hurt but they'd survived. As CS Martin rushed in the doorway, disrupting the moment, Valentine shifted his perspective, he knew Jade and Darry would be all right, they had each other.

'Right, Finnie, on your feet,' said the DI.

Grant Finnie turned around and placed his hands on the back of his head – the move seemed practised like he had been in preparation for this moment for some time. 'He's better dead, you know,' he said.

Valentine longed to agree but the words evaded him.

He'd sworn to remove murderers from society, no matter how much he agreed with this one's cause, it wasn't his job to sympathise, or even try to understand him. He grabbed Finnie's wrists and led him towards the door. Outside DS McNeil was waiting with handcuffs to lead Finnie away to the Land Rover that had just arrived, lights flashing. As Valentine handed him over, he made no struggle, just slopped off behind the DS, head bowed.

'Are you OK, Jade?' said Valentine.

She nodded through her tears, she was still clinging to her brother; CS Martin stood nearby, offering a comforting hug that appeared out of character.

'What's going to happen to us now?' said Jade.

'Hard to say. There'll be questions, lots of them, but the first step is to get you checked out by a doctor.'

'There's money in there, Finnie brought it. It was for me, to go away and get it taken away.'

Darry looked up at the DI, spoke: 'What'll happen to her?'

'It's not for me to say, but your sister will be taken care of, Darry, you don't need to worry about that. She's a victim in all of this, we'll look after her, there's systems in place to make everything as stress-free as possible for her.' Valentine eased them towards the car. 'Come on, it's getting dark, let's get inside and get some warmth into the pair of you, we don't need to clear this mess up tonight.'

As CS Martin led Darry and Jade up the path at the side of the bothy she summoned Valentine with a backward nod. 'Bob, I just took a call from Ally, the MoD chucked a fit when he told them about the case. I'd say there's a better than good shot at reopening the murder allegations against Tulloch from Afghanistan.'

'Shame it's come too late for the whistle-blower, not to mention Jade and Darry.'

'Still, it's something.'

'Almost justice.'

More police cars were arriving, DS McCormack was in the same Astra she'd left in earlier. She stood on the edge of the bothy looking at Valentine as he retrieved the holdall containing the money Finnie had taken from Leask at the Meat Hangers. The sky was dark but luminous behind the DS as she called out, 'Are you all right, Bob?'

'Why wouldn't I be?'

'We had a running commentary on the radio from McNeil.'

'Oh, right.' He drew level with McCormack.

'I was worried about you.'

Valentine let down the bag, it rested between them on the shaley path towards the glen. 'This weighs a ton, must be a fair amount of cash in there.'

'Are you tempted to run away with it?'

'I wouldn't get very far.'

'Is that because you're getting on a bit?' She suppressed a laugh.

'No,' he said. 'It's because we've missed the last ferry home.'

'Well, that means Dino's budget's going to get another battering tonight.'

'I'd say you're right once again, Sylvia.'